Bozo

The Circus Prince

First published in hardcopy format in 2013.

All name, characters, places, organization business and events are either the product of the author's imagination or are used fictitiously. Any resemblance to actual persons, living or dead, is purely coincidental.

For Mary, my Oscar

From the Beginning

"No way," said Bozo as he stamped his feet and folded his arms.

"Bozo, you have to go to school tomorrow," said his mother, Marija.

"I'm not going. I don't care. I can go to bed early without my dinner for the next year as punishment. It's better than going to school. I am not going and that's it," said Bozo.

"Bozo," said Marija sharply, "we've been having this conversation for the last twenty minutes and the entire summer holidays. You are going to school tomorrow and that's the end of it."

"No I'm not," he shouted back.

Marija rolled her eyes to heaven. “Franjo,” she called for her husband.

“What’s wrong?” asked Franjo as he walked into the room.

“He won’t go to school tomorrow,” she replied.

“Oh, not this again,” said Franjo as he too rolled his eyes to heaven. He sat on Bozo’s bed to reason with him. “Bozo, you’re going to have to learn to stand up for yourself. Tell those boys to get lost, leave you alone, and find someone else to pick on.”

“No,” Bozo replied.

“No?” asked Franjo in shock. “Have we not been practicing this for the whole summer?”

“I SAID NO. I am not going to school tomorrow and I am NOT standing up for myself,” replied Bozo firmly.

"Why not?" asked Franjo

Bozo wouldn't answer. He stuck out his bottom lip and stared at the floor.

"Bozo, answer your father when he asks you a question," said Marija.

Bozo still wouldn't answer and he kept his arms folded and stared at the floor.

"Bozo, what is the matter now?" asked Marija, who knew she should have asked the question softly, but she was losing her patience. "You were fine all summer. You were going to stand up to those boys and you were even looking forward to it. Now what?"

"Because I can't. I'm not able to," said Bozo, now looking up at the ceiling beams, and across at the stone walls. Anywhere! But he avoided eye contact with his parents in case he started to cry.

“Not able to stand up for yourself? You’re doing a pretty good job of that now,” said Franjo.

“That’s different,” he responded.

“That’s right. We’re only your parents. Don’t worry about us. No need to be afraid of us. Sure, we only feed you and cloth you and make sure you’re safe,” said Franjo.

“It’s not the same,” replied Bozo

“How is it not the same?” Franjo was not only tired but he was now confused.

“I don’t know. I can’t explain it. It doesn’t make sense. I open my mouth and nothing, I mean *nothing*, comes out. And it’s not like my mind goes blank. I know I should say something and I’ve practiced like we said for weeks - the whole summer - but I can’t do it. I can’t even talk. I can't even say 'leave me alone.' I can't even stammer a sarcastic 'Okay, here you go, enjoy your, sorry, *my* lunch.'"

Bozo had two big disadvantages. The first was that he was the smallest in the class, so he was always picked on.

The second was that everyone else in the class had a brother or cousin who would defend them whenever they were attacked.

When the Mafia ganged up on one of the boys in the playground, it was as though a secret whistle was blown all around the school. All the cousins and brothers immediately dropped what they were doing and ran to the aid of their family member under attack. This was the only road to survival – family watched out for family, but friends were left to fend for themselves.

Bozo had no relatives to come to his rescue in the school yard. He was an only child. His mother was an only child and so too was his father, who was raised in a circus community. Unfortunately, Bozo had not grown an inch over the summer. But he could punch harder, jump higher and he had razor-sharp moves that would flatten even the strongest member of the Mafia with just one slick karate chop.

“Your mother and I have been into the school to talk to your principal about this countless times. All of this stopped during the few weeks before the summer holidays, didn’t it?” Franjo was rubbing his forehead with his hands.

“Yes, but ...” Bozo stammered.

“But nothing, Bozo. We’ve been through this every day, EVERY DAY, for the entire summer holidays and for months before that last year. What more can we do? We practiced all of your self-defense and karate moves.

You know to stay with people in the schoolyard so that they can't single you out.

We've gone through it all, scene by scene, scenario by scenario.

They won't touch you. Your new teacher will be warned about this and if they lay one finger on you, you are to tell your new teacher and they will be expelled immediately. They're on their last warning."

"But Dad, it's not like that. They're clever. They don't pick on me in front of teachers."

"What's the matter here?" asked Bozo's grandmother, who could hear the commotion in the bedroom.

"I'm not going to school tomorrow. I'm just not! And neither of you can make me," he said.

"Oh come on, Bozo. You're nine now. You need to toughen up. You have to face this. You know that there are no other schools that we can send you to - they're either too expensive or too far away, and you have to go to school or else you'll be breaking the law. And you don't want to get in trouble with the police, do you?"

"But Dad, I'm going to join you in the circus and become your assistant. Remember you said that Mr. Edwards is in town and if he sees us he can turn us into circus superstars? You'll be Franjo the King of the Circus, and I'll be Bozo the Circus Prince."

Franjo stared at him and whispered firmly from the corner of his mouth, "I told you not to mention that in front of your mother and your grandmother."

"Oh, a prince now, are you? Oh, I see," said Grandmother. "That's clever. I can see the front page of the local paper now: *Boy, 9, leaves school to join penniless father in circus royalty, sorry, circus poverty.*

The only solution he sees to all of this mess is to start dreaming of becoming a famous circus Superstar again. Can't you see this boy is not living in the real world? Such nonsense you and your people are teaching this poor boy."

"What nonsense are you talking about? Anyway, you *are* my 'people'. You're my family, for heaven's sake," said Franjo. Franjo was the King of the Circus, something he was very proud of. He had worked hard for this title, which he earned by being the best circus performer not just in the village of Slavlov, or the country of Vladislav, but in the whole of Europe. He had gone head to head with many of the great circus performers in live showdowns in front of hundreds of performers, but every time the audience had cheered Franjo to be the greatest. Being his son, Bozo was now the Circus Prince.

“Huh, by marriage only. I am not part of that circus hocus-pocus, psychedelic, flying-thingies rubbish. I am educated and refined and cultured. Bozo, you will be too. Your father being the Circus King has brought this family nothing but disappointment. He let Marija think that she would live a life of fun and entertainment and travel the world. And where did you travel to? The end of my driveway. A free site for him to build a tiny cottage. This was *not* the life that Marija was destined for."

"Mother, that's enough," said Marija.

Franjo hung upside down from the beams on the ceiling just to annoy her even more.

"I mean what gentleman of any pedigree, with some sort of common sense would turn upside down and hang from a beam when I speak?"

"One that is bored maybe?"

Even Bozo cracked a smile at his father's cheekiness.

"Okay, you two, cut it out," said Marija, trying to referee between her mother and her husband.

Franjo swung down from the ceiling beams and jumped to attention. He may not have taken his mother-in-law seriously but he definitely respected and loved his wife.

“Now come on, Bozo. There is nothing to be worried about. This year is going to be different,” reasoned Marija.

“Your mother’s right. Think of it this way: you don’t ever have to speak to those boys. There are only a few times in the day that they can bother you: right before class, lunchtime and on the way home from school.

So here’s our plan. You arrive into school one minute after the bell rings. That way they will all be in class, in their seats, and you sit in front of the teacher so they can’t touch you. At lunchtime make sure as you’re walking out you sandwich yourself between the two tallest boys in the class and stay only in the top of the schoolyard, right in front of the staffroom, so that if any trouble starts you scream and the teachers will be out straight away. We sewed a small video recorder into the top of your jacket pocket, with just a small hole cut out for the lens. The other top pocket in your jacket is filled with batteries so you won't run out for a few months and we can show it to the principal afterwards. And lastly, just before the bell rings. I have told your principal to tell your new teacher that you have to leave one minute before everybody else. This gives you enough time to get your bike and cycle as fast as you can out of the school gates and away before the rest of the class leaves.

"I'll walk into school with you, dear, up to the front door," suggested Marija, "and I'll tell those boys myself to leave you alone."

"Mom, come on, that's embarrassing! No one will want to talk to me then. They'll hate me even more," said Bozo.

"I agree, honey, that's a bad idea. It just gives them even more reason to tease him," said Franjo. "And don't start standing up for anyone else, Bozo. You're a good fighter - you even knocked me down a few times.

So if they do start to kick you, you can fight for yourself, but don't fight anyone else's battles. You have enough to do to look after yourself. Look, Bozo, you may not be tall but you are a fighter, you are strong and fit and you can outsmart any of these guys in your sleep. You're fitter than you were before the summer, you are stronger and you are smarter. I believe you can do this, okay?" Franjo asked in an effort to cheer him up.

"Okay," said Bozo, as meek as a mouse.

"Okay?" Franjo asked once more, raising his voice to put some passion into Bozo's belly. "Remember what we talked about, Bozo. You are fitter, you are faster, you are better, you are the best. You are a man, not a mouse. Come on, lift your head up, say it again."

Feeling a lot better, and with far more passion, Bozo responded, "I am fitter, I am faster, I am better, I am the best!"

Here We Go Again

The bell of Slavlov National School for Boys chimed nine times for nine o'clock and all the pupils scurried into class for their first day of term on the 3rd of September 1995. Slavlov was a small farming village high in the hills of Vladislav in Eastern Europe, beside the Adriatic Sea. The school was built of local stone and had a thatched roof and three classrooms.

The first day of school brought an air of nervousness to the school, but no one was as nervous as Mrs. Butcher. It was her first time teaching in this school.

She walked apologetically into the classroom,

nodding hello to a class of twenty-five nine-year-old boys who were watching her every move and gesture. They were sizing her up. Was this a teacher who was going to make them shiver in their boots? Or was she a teacher they could play tricks on and who would let them play games on each other during class? She took eleven steps across the classroom to the wooden desk just beside the window and in front of the blackboard. It was enough for the classroom jury to come to their verdict: a pushover.

"Hello, everyone," Mrs. Butcher said very quietly, nodding her head as she walked to her desk and dropped her books onto the floor. "Oh I am sorry," she said so softly that no one heard her.

She was nothing like the butcher her name implied. She was a mild-mannered lady, and not just in her beautiful speaking voice and expensive jewellery. She was in fact a descendant of English royalty. She never boasted about the fact, but it was implied in everything about her. To the locals she carelessly mentioned that her servants had cooked an amazing meal for the ambassador of some foreign land, and it was hard to miss her enormous expensive car and its chauffeur, which looked completely out of place in the small village of Slavlov. Most of the families did not own a car and made their money working hard on their small farms. Mrs. Butcher had travelled to Slavlov and simply fell in love with its charm and simplicity. She had convinced her husband to stop working so hard and to live a more normal life for a while in the countryside, and Vladislav was the only Eastern European country where fluent English was spoken.

"It's been a long time since I was a teacher, so you're going to have to be patient with me," she explained, trying to put her class at ease and trying to buy herself some empathy.

"I give her one month," said one of boys in the classroom sitting at the back of the class as he leaned over to his two other friends. He knew the hassle these boys had caused previous teachers and none of them had lasted more than two months.

"I'll give her until the end of the week," one of the other boys replied.

"I'll give *us* until the end of the week," sighed

another as he cupped his face with his hands in despair of yet another year of the Mafia causing terror with no teacher strong enough to take charge.

The second bell had chimed and, to plan, Bozo skidded through the gates of the schoolyard and zoomed past the window. Keeping to the strategy he and his father had agreed, he threw his small rusty bike over the school wall into a dumping ground so that the Mafia wouldn't either steal it or slash its tyres.

When Bozo cycled through the gates of the school, all of the terror, worry and panic came flooding back into his mind. His heart started to beat so loudly that he felt it throbbing in his throat. *Oh no,* he thought, *cottonmouth again. I hate this.*

His mouth had dried and his whole body shook with fear.

He could even feel his lip start to shiver with terror. The only way to stop it was to start not living in the real world.

For the last few pedals before parking his bike and running into class, Bozo imagined himself and his father as rich and famous circus superstars.

Walking past a sea of photographers and screaming fans; they would sign autographs and be chauffeured to their yacht, where the Mafia could only look on jealously. Every day he dreamt of himself surrounded by butlers, fine food and entertainers as the Mafia polished his shoes or scrubbed the floors of his castle.

Would I give them food to eat?

He pondered. Some days he thought he would, others maybe not. No, he would do what they did to him and all the other boys in the class: eat his meal in front of them as they looked on hungrily.

Taking a deep breath, Bozo walked into the musty corridor. The familiar smell brought back every horrible feeling from the year before as he turned the corner and slowly walked into the room, praying that his teacher would be a big strong hulk of a man who wouldn't take any nonsense.

Glancing around the room, he searched for the boys who made his life a misery. And there they were. The three biggest, tallest, ugliest boys in the class. The Mafia.

They were sitting at the back, keeping watch

over everyone and he just knew that they would antagonise each pupil just out of earshot of the new teacher.

Just my luck, thought Bozo as he searched the class for a free seat. The only seat that remained was right beside the ringleader himself, Vito. Breathing deeply, he straightened his shoulders, just as his father had showed him, and held his head high, avoiding the piercing gaze of the Mafia vultures eying their prey.

“I am better than these losers. I will beat them,” he chanted repeatedly to himself. I am fitter. I am faster. I am bet -”

Vito kicked his shin and Bozo landed face first on the floor with a thunderous noise.

Bozo’s shin, chin and arm were very sore, but

he wasn't about to let any of these losers know that he was in pain. He fought back his tears. "Think of wardrobes," his dad always told to stop him from crying. It was a way of thinking about something unemotional to fight back the tears. But there weren't any wardrobes in the classroom, so Bozo counted the nine panes of glass and the twelve books on the bookshelf to control his tears. His father had taught him that trick - count chairs, fingers, pictures, anything at all to stop crying. He reached for his video recorder to see if it had caught the evidence, but it had slipped out of his pocket and slid across the floor.

"Loser," said Vito, the tallest of the Mafia members, under his breath, just loudly enough for Bozo to hear but for the teacher not to.

Bozo was furious. His first introduction to the new school year in which he wouldn't let these bullies ruin his life, and this was how it started.

"Loser," Bozo belted back at the top of his lungs with every ounce of fight he could muster. Teacher or no teacher, school or no school, Bozo was no longer going to be bullied by these creeps.

"Oh my word!" Mrs. Butcher put her hand to her mouth, as though horrified that a cute little boy could utter such a bad word.

She wasn't the only one. As angry as he was, Bozo had surprised himself. His mother was very strict that he not call anyone names, and this was the first time he had disobeyed her rule.

"I am shocked," said Mrs. Butcher, "and very

disappointed."

Oh, come on, thought Bozo. Shocked he understood; he had shocked himself. But disappointed? She didn't even know him.

"The seven year olds are in the next room. Give them your fake disappointment," he felt like saying. But he was in enough trouble already, so he kept that one to himself.

"Vito," said Mrs. Butcher to the ringleader, "are you okay?"

His lip started to tremble.

He's a good actor, thought Bozo.

"I can't believe someone would hate me like that, Miss," said Vito as he started to cry.

"He tripped me!" Bozo exclaimed, desperate for Mrs. Butcher to see that Vito was the bully here.

"I did not!" Vito looked horrified by the suggestion.

"He did trip me, I swear," promised Bozo. In the circus world, to swear on your word is an absolute guarantee that you are telling the truth.

To do so and tell a lie meant your life would be cursed forever. But Mrs. Butcher wasn't part of the circus world, so this gesture was useless. Vito started to cry again.

"Come now, Vito," said Mrs. Butcher as she put her arm on his shoulders to comfort him. "Did anyone else in the class see Vito trip him?" The whole class had seen it, but nobody was brave enough to come to his rescue. *We aren't related*, thought Bozo with resignation.

"What is your name, young man?" Mrs. Butcher

asked firmly.

"Bozo, Miss," he replied sheepishly. Bozo's heart was on the floor. He was gutted. Gutted because Vito was out to get him this year, just like every other year, and despite all of his training during the summer, he had fallen at the first hurdle.

While Bozo had spent the summer practicing martial arts, Vito had been practicing fake crying, and Vito's strategy was winning.

Secondly, and even worse, his teacher was a total weakling. She would not be able to see through these phonies. He was going to have to up his game.

"Well Bozo, you have made this boy very sad," she continued. "This is not a nice way to start the year, and I do regret that as punishment you will have detention during lunch hour every day this month."

That was a tough punishment on the first day of school, by anyone's standards. The whole class seemed to reassess just how much of a weakling Mrs. Butcher was after all.

Dejected, Bozo picked up his bag and sat in his seat. If he was expected to go through another school year like this, he was going to have to think of a way out of Slavlov fast!

Let the Magic Happen

Mrs. Butcher had taken the class outside for a nature walk to ease them into the start of the year. Bozo was not invited because of what had happened earlier that morning and he spent the time alone in the classroom, where the teacher had set him some work to do. He had passed the hour not living in the real world and imagining his life as a circus superstar. He had come to the conclusion that every great circus performer needed an assistant. All the greats have assistants, and if he was going to be great then he needed one, too.

The next morning Mrs. Butcher walked into class with her hands on the shoulder of a timid boy who walked shyly in front of her. He had black hair and wore a pair of brown jeans and a blue shirt that was buttoned right up to the neck. He was wearing a pair of black-rimmed glasses with lenses so thick they made his eyes look twice the size of everyone else's. They looked like they were bulging out of his head. But more unusual than that, he was cradling a bird in his hands as tightly as a mother would hold on to a newborn baby. Bozo wondered why a bird would be allowed into the class.

The bell rang again and the class bulldozed their way into the classroom, oblivious to Mrs. Butcher and the new student, who were bumped so many times that they nearly fell over. Of course, she said nothing to reprimand them.

Once the class settled she said, "May I have your attention, class?"

She really is very posh, thought Bozo, who was not used to such formality.

"This is our new friend, Andre." She paused before she said his name, and then said it very slowly.

He looked up nervously over his glasses. He was absolutely terrified. Bozo noticed that the teacher said everything much slower to him than she had to anyone else in the class that morning.

"Won't you all be nice to Andre?" she said, again slowing down when she mentioned his name.

That was an unusual thing to say, thought Bozo. No teacher ever says that when they are introducing a new pupil.

"Bring it on," said Vito under his breath, delighted with the new prey to bully.

Bozo felt a slight twinge of relief that Vito would find someone else to pick on, although he couldn't help but feel sorry for this poor sucker. *He looks like he wouldn't say boo to a mouse, he's so shy.*

"Andre will be colouring in pictures for our history and geography lessons this morning," Mrs. Butcher continued. Bozo thought this was another unusual thing to say.

"That's not fair," good old Vito piped up.

He never lets up, thought Bozo. *Why is he always causing trouble?*

"Not fair," agreed Sonny, Vito's sidekick, interrupting Bozo's thoughts. Mrs. Butcher just ignored their complaints and Andre took his seat right in front of Bozo.

During geography class, Mrs. Butcher asked Andre a question. “Okay now, Andre,” she began, pointing to the map on the wall, “we all live in this county. What ... is ... the ... name ... of ... this ... country?” Mrs. Butcher said it slowly so that he would understand.

Andre said nothing.

“Come on now, Andre. We live in this country,” she said again.

The boys started to snigger. “France,” one of them whispered, knowing it was the wrong answer.

“France, Miss?” Andre replied, unsure of whether it was the correct answer or not.

The class erupted in laughter because it was

such an easy question. Bozo was just relieved that for once he wasn't the one being picked on.

Andre blushed.

"No, not France, Andre. Try again," she said, trying to encourage him. But he buried his head in his chest, next to his bird.

"Try again, Andre," she repeated, but Andre ignored her.

"Andre is very good magician," said Mrs. Butcher overenthusiastically. "Show the boys some of your tricks," she continued.

This piqued Bozo's attention. *Another performer in the class*, he thought. But he was very doubtful that Andre was any good. It wasn't like he was full of confidence and showmanship.

Andre stood up sheepishly, although he was definitely more at ease doing his magic trick than when he had been asked a geography question.

His bird flew onto his left shoulder, taking part in the act. Andre took a coin out of his pocket and placed it in the palm of his hand, while holding a pen in his other hand.

"I am going to make this coin disappear with three waves of this pen," he explained. Holding the coin in his clinched fist, he tapped it with his pen, his bird tweeting with each wave.

"One, two, three." But on the third tap the pen disappeared.

"Hang on; I think I got that the wrong way around. Maybe it's the pen that's supposed to disappear. Now where did I leave it?" The bird jumped onto his right shoulder, removed the pen from behind his ear with his beak and gave it to Andre.

“But the thing is, when the pen comes back, the coin disappears.” Tapping his fist with the pen three times, Andre opened his palm to reveal that the coin had gone. His bird flew over to his left hand side and dipped his beak into Andre’s pocket. He removed the coin and gave it to Andre.

“That’s excellent! Well done, Andre.” Mrs. Butcher was the only one to clap. The class were amused, but it didn’t get him off the hook for being teacher’s pet.

Bozo was beginning to like this guy. He could be his circus assistant. He knew Andre needed to take things a little bit slower than the rest of the boys in the class. But that was okay - sometimes Bozo needed to do the same.

BANG! The sound of an explosion in the distance filled the room

“What was that?” asked Bozo and his classmates.

“Everyone be calm,” said Mrs. Butcher, who looked like she was the most shaken from the sound.

“Miss, is it true that there are soldiers who are going to come to our village from other countries and kill us all?” said one of the boys.

“What?” said Bozo, in shock. He quickly looked around the class to see if everyone else had heard the same thing.

“Of course not. Where did you hear such a thing?” Mrs. Butcher asked as though it was the most outrageous thing she had ever heard.

"It's true, Miss. My father said it last night to his friends. We're going to war and we're all going to be soldiers," said another student.

"War ..."

"War?"

"We're going to war?" The class was in a panic, with boys shouting questions at no one in particular.

"Oh no, of course not," Mrs. Butcher reassured them. "Now can everyone please -"

The bell rang for lunchtime.

Bozo had detention so he had to stay in the classroom. All the boys left, but Andre did not. He sat on his own, eating his sandwich and feeding his bird.

"Hi, I'm Bozo." Bozo introduced himself with a

half-smile.

Andre just continued to eat his bread.

“Where are you from?” Bozo asked, slightly offended that Andre didn’t answer him the first time, but still he persisted.

Andre still said nothing

“I was only trying to be your friend, you know. You’re going to have to have friends around here if you want to stay alive.”

Andre’s bird tweeted at him.

“See, even your bird wants to be my friend,” Bozo said. At this point, he felt like he was just talking to himself. “Do you have any friends?” he asked.

Andre lowered his head. He looked sad.

“I don’t have that many either,” said Bozo, who didn’t seem as bothered. He asked the most important question of all: “Do you have any brothers or cousins in this school?”

Andre’s silence spoke very loudly.

“Neither do I,” said Bozo, more bothered about that one. He couldn’t help feeling badly that Andre looked so sad. “Why are you so sad?” he asked. Even though he knew it was rude, he still was dying to find out.

“Don’t know,” said Andre, shrugging his shoulders.

“Come on, you must know,” probed Bozo.

“Because I’m different,” Andre answered honestly.

“Why do you think you’re different?” asked Bozo, although he wished he hadn’t. He already thought Andre was different.

“I can’t run as fast as everybody else.”

At least he's not acting, thought Bozo. He liked that. It was a good start.

"Yeah, I know what you mean." Bozo could relate to him on that one. "What's your bird's name?" he asked, intrigued.

"Oscar," Andre answered as Oscar flew down from the ceiling and landed on Bozo's shoulder. He started to playfully nip him with his beak.

"I think he wants to be your friend," said Andre, laughing. It was the first smile Andre had broken all day.

"If Oscar is your friend, can you be my friend, too?" Andre asked, as though this was the only way to become friends with him.

"Okay," Bozo agreed. "Is he your imaginary friend? I used to have one of those years ago." Bozo secretly thought it was quite childish for a boy of nine to still have an imaginary friend.

"He's not imaginary," said Andre, almost insulted by the suggestion. "He's not imaginary; you can see him."

"But he's just a bird," said Bozo honestly. He thought they could be honest with each other.

"He's not just a bird," explained Andre. "He was a present from my daddy. And Daddy's in heaven so he tells Oscar to look after me, and he does."

That sentence cut deeply with Bozo. He was stunned. Bozo imagined how he would feel if his father died and he had no friends and could not run as fast as everyone and always felt different. It made him so sad that he felt a twinge in his heart and he could feel the sides of his mouth tremble and curl downwards and his eyes fill with tears. He fought desperately not to cry. He *hated* for anyone to see him cry and this was the second time today and he hadn't done it all summer. He begged himself not to cry but the tears streamed down his cheeks.

He looked to the ground and tried desperately to think of something quickly that would stop his crying. Like the pattern on the carpet, or counting the stripes on his runners - anything that would make the tears stop streaming and his nose stop running. But nothing worked.

"Did you hear that sound?" Bozo pretended that he had heard a noise just outside the door

"What sound?" replied Andre. He hadn't heard anything and had noticed that Bozo kept his head down.

"Just outside the door," said Bozo as he walked out into the empty corridor where nobody could see him. He pretended to be checking out the noise, while he wiped his eyes dry with some tissues and cleaned his nose. He just felt so sorry for Andre.

Taking deep breaths, Bozo heard his father's words echo in his mind: "In order to have a friend, you need to be a friend."

Bozo hated that Andre was lonely and different and had no friends. He hated that Andre had an imaginary friend just like he had years ago because he was small and didn't have any cousins, brothers or sisters.

I'm nearly a man now, thought Bozo. Even though he had only grown a little, it was something, and something was better than nothing. At least Bozo had his mom and dad and grandmother and annoying neighbours who always pinched his checks and laughed for absolutely no reason when they spoke to him. This was different. Andre's father was dead. Bozo was still wiping away his tears at the thought of his father dying. He decided he could change one thing. From that moment, Bozo was going to be Andre's best friend. Bozo would be his protector. They would be a team, just the two of them – well, two and a half if you counted Oscar. From here on Bozo and Andre were going to be best friends. Bozo thought about that for a few moments and it made his sad eyes glitter. Wearing a beaming smile, Bozo turned and walked over to Andre and Oscar. He straightened his shoulders and stuck out his chest the same way as his father did when he had a business deal.

"I have a proposition for you," said Bozo, mimicking his father talking to a banker when he had a business idea.

"A what?" said Andre.

"A proposition," Bozo repeated.

"What's a prop ... prop ... magician?" asked Andre, without a clue what that big word meant.

"We used to have one at home, but the wheel fell off," Bozo joked. This was another thing his father always said when people used a big word that he didn't understand. It always got a big laugh.

"What?" Andre still didn't get the joke.

"Let's be best friends. Plus, I need a circus

assistant. Are you interested in the position?" said Bozo, dying to get to the point. "By the way I'm a circus prince."

"A prince? Wow - a real prince!" said Andre.

"Yes, a real prince. You don't have any friends or cousins and neither do I. And let's face it, we need to stick together around here. We could be best friends. What do you think?" said Bozo.

Andre's face beamed. "Really? Wow! This is better than any birthday present, any Christmas present, even better than a new bicycle," said Andre. "Really? You want to be my friend?"

Andre's smile beamed from the bottom of his heart. It was the most sincere, most willing response.

Bozo could feel his eyes welling up again. He

realised how much it meant to Andre to have a friend. He was sad that this was yet another thing Andre had never had, and he was so pleased that he had made him happy. Not only that, but Bozo was going to have a best friend, too.

"Let's shake on it," said Bozo, who put out his hand like his father does. Andre stood up with Oscar on his shoulder.

Andre gripped Bozo's hand firmly as Oscar chirped loudly. Bozo wasn't too sure if it was the sunshine gleaming through the glass that made Oscar glisten, but as Oscar chirped with excitement around the classroom, he could have sworn he saw Oscar glow a golden light.

"It's a deal," said Bozo, copying another thing he heard his father say to the bankers. "By the way, we're going to be really famous circus superstars – you, me and my dad," said Bozo with absolute certainty.

Same Old, Same Old

The afternoon of Bozo's first day back in school, Marija was hanging the washing on the clothesline when she heard a familiar laugh in the distance. Slightly confused, she couldn't figure out where the noise came from. She pulled back the white linen blanket she had just hung on the washing line and looked in front of her. Searching between the trees in the forest, she couldn't see anything unusual, just the tall trunks of the trees, providing shelter for her house. Just to be sure, she looked behind her, her eyes searching the back of her small cottage. There was no one there, just

Grouse the sheepdog and an old bicycle. The divided door was closed at the bottom to keep out the chickens that clucked around the yard. The top part was open to let in the still afternoon air and glorious sunshine.

"It was probably nothing," she said to herself dismissively. After all, she was in a hurry to get all her washing done before the heat of the day kicked in. It was one of the hottest days of the year, and from the hours of noon until three she would have to stay in the shade. She continued hanging the clothes on the line. Most of the chores were done and it was just about time to make herself a well-earned cup of coffee.

"I do hope Bozo does not turn out like his father," said Grandmother as she sat deep in thought, somehow unaware and unconcerned that she had made the statement out loud.

Marija gave her a sharp look. She counted to ten in her mind, a technique she had been practicing around her mother for quite some time. The urge to launch into a full-blown argument passed.

“Bozo is a very talented boy and, whatever career he decides to take in life, I have no doubt he will be very successful. I’ll support him every step of the way,” Marija said matter-of-factly. She intended a polite response that would defend her son without offending her mother.

Of course Marija’s polite, intelligent response was wasted on her mother, who barely listened.

“I mean, I really hope that all that nonsense

with the circus is out of his system now. I'd like him to be a lawyer. He would be a good lawyer. He's articulate, warm, and very likable. He gets all of that from me. People always say that I'm very intelligent. I've always been careful to set a good example around Bozo. It's clear my hard work is paying off." Again, Grandmother said this staring into the woods as though deep in thought about Bozo's future career.

Grandmother didn't bother with hidden intent. She just said it right out. She was too old to be bothered about offending people. Marija had become immune to her mother's self-praise.

"Any chance you could help me hang up the washing, Mom?" she asked, changing the subject. Her question was mostly rhetorical.

Her mother had been sitting watching her do chores for the past few days without offering any help.

"I would love to, you know I would. But my hip is very sore. Today I can barely stand up."

Marija counted to ten again and started humming to herself, not wanting to instigate an argument. Despite her annoyance, her mother had been good to her and would never let her and Franjo go without. It pained them, but they were often forced to ask her mother for some money to see them through the winter. Her mother would always oblige, often giving up little luxuries she was looking forward to herself. However, as Marija and Franjo were well aware, there's no such a thing as a free dinner. And while they couldn't afford to repay her, there was a tax on the kindness she gifted them. That tax was charged every so often in cutting remarks directed at their family. It was times like this that Marija missed having another sibling to share the burden. A half hour had passed and Marija was bending down to pick up her empty basket when she heard a faint noise in the distance.

“Did you hear that?” Marija turned to her mother, who was resting in the corner of the yard, just beside the back of the cottage. She had woken with a start and was resting at the wrought iron picnic table. The heat of the sun had sent her into a doze, and the only thing that was disturbing her peaceful day was a buzzing fly that had been trying to land on her nose.

"Hear what? I didn't hear anything but the noise of this annoying fly that keeps trying to eat me," said Grandmother as she shooed away the fly with the back of her hand.

Grandmother eventually won the fight and the buzzing fly had buzzed off and was trying to land on the nose of Grouse. The sheepdog started a similar fight.

Marija had put her hand on the handle of the half door when the laugher bellowed again. This time Marija, Grandmother and Grouse stopped in shock and looked towards the woods in search of the familiar sound.

Marija didn't know what reached her first, the sight of her nine-year-old Bozo bouncing up above the trees or the boy's screams of hysterical laughter. He looked to be trampolining from somewhere deep in the forest and was being catapulted high above the trees into the sky.

“Bozo!” Marija belted with every ounce of anger she could muster as she slammed down her basket and pegs.

“FRANJOOOooo!” she shouted. She was annoyed with Bozo, but she knew that her husband had something to do with this. The noise echoed around the farmyard so loudly that Grouse stood up on his paws as though taking direction from his master. He was on duty to protect and without instruction he briskly followed Marija as she marched into the woods, screaming the name of her husband and only child. Grouse was barking with every word she uttered.

Grandmother stood up immediately and walked a few paces behind Marija, almost forgetting that she had a sore hip and that she needed a walking stick. Every ounce of anger and frustration pumping through Marija's body was displayed in her clenched fists and her pursed lips, her eyes narrowing to home in on her prey.

As Marija marched through the woods, Grandmother shouted after her, "Well I'm not surprised. He will never learn. That man is a danger to his own child. I told you, but you wouldn't listen to me. He's useless! Why can't he get a real job?"

Marija was too angry to react to her mother's words and so annoyed that she almost agreed with her. She had promised never to give out about Franjo to her mother, but today she was about to break that promise. Grandmother's words became more distant as Marija stormed deeper into the woods following the laughter. Her skirt caught on barbed wire and thorns, and her feet stumbled along the uneven ground that was dotted with badger holes.

Why on earth would they go so far into the forest? she wondered. But the thought had barely occurred to her when she came to the conclusion: Franjo was teaching Bozo *another* forbidden circus trick and they had to escape far into the woods to conceal it from her. The more she tripped and stumbled along into the woods, the madder she became. If Franjo had gone to this much effort to conceal this trick from her, then she knew two things. One, he knew he was doing something wrong; and two, it must be a very dangerous trick.

The bellowing laughter grew clearer and clearer. Marija could make out bodies in the distance, and the picture was unfolding.

Franjo had done it again. He couldn't help himself. He had rested one end of the red pole twenty feet long and about six inches wide on the cup of the two branches of a thick sturdy tree, securing it with a thick rope. The other end of the red pole was held by Franjo on his shoulder. Bozo was bouncing up and down on the middle of the pole. On the ground were old mattresses, pillows and cushions in case Bozo fell. Bozo held his arms out in a perfectly straight line, his head held high for optimal balance. Bozo bounced on the long, narrow pole, springing him into the air almost twenty feet high, higher than the tips of the tallest trees.

“Look, Dad, I’m flying! I’m flying!” Bozo felt like he was flying to the top of the world and back again.

Bozo’s body may have been on top of the world, but Marija’s temper was at boiling point. She stood frozen in anger as she watched this act of Russian roulette. One false move and Bozo could have broken a leg or an arm or even his back.

For a split second, Marija considered not screaming, in case they both got a fright and Bozo fell by accident. But her temper decided otherwise. “What is going on here?” that split second had passed and her annoyance was victorious over logic.

Her neck was bright red with anger. Even Grouse knew that these two were in big trouble and took a few steps away from Marija.

Bozo looked at his mother. He knew he was in trouble so he jumped to the ground.

Franjo knew he had broken his promise and he was in big trouble. Even bigger trouble than the time she had smelled something burning and looked out the window at Bozo and Franjo juggling flaming sticks. Or the time she was coming home from town and saw Bozo on a unicycle, cycling on a piece of rope strung high between two trees.

“Franjo, what are you thinking?” Marija exclaimed. “Bozo is not to do any circus acts!”

“But Mom, this is all I’ve ever wanted to do,” said Bozo, trying to reason with her. “We’re going to be famous after this show. And rich! And travel the world!"

"Listen to all that nonsense. See what you're doing?" Marija shouted at Franjo.

"What am I doing?" Franjo demanded. "What's wrong with him being in the show on Friday?"

"He thinks that we're going to be superstars. Have you ever heard such nonsense?" she scolded.

"Oh, come on. What's wrong with that? The boy's allowed to dream isn't he? He's a child for heaven's sake," said Franjo.

"Dream? Dream!" She looked directly at Franjo. "That's all we have Franjo. For ten years you've promised me that we would travel the world with your circus and we haven't moved. We haven't even been on a holiday. We can barely afford to eat and I'm sick of it."

"Darling, I know, but he is a talented acrobat. He could be the best in the world. Plus, this show is in four days and it could be our big break," Franjo reasoned. They had had this argument many times before.

"Please, Mother, please," begged Bozo. "Just this once?"

"It'll be the last time, I promise," said Franjo, resigning himself to the fact that he needed to give up his dream and start looking for a real job, one that would last all year round, something he had promised to do lots of times before.

"Fine, Franjo. But you must promise me this is the last show and after this you will get a job - a real one that fixes the leak in the roof, feeds us good food in the winter and provides some nice new clothes."

"Of course, my darling," said Franjo, putting his arm lovingly around her shoulder.

Besties

Of course, not everyone in the country of Vladislav was poor. Over the mountains of Slavlov, miles away from bouncing Bozo was the Pearl of the Adriatic Sea - a small but fabulous village called Port Alexandrov that held some of the most expensive and impressive yachts in the world, owned by some of the richest and most powerful people in the world.

Franjo and Bozo were in their rusty old van going to the harbour. They worked there cleaning the magnificent yachts. Tonight they had Andre as their helper.

They pulled up to Andre's home. It was a caravan. It was small, silver and it had some rust along the edges but it looked very clean and tidy from the outside. A pleasant, tall, slim lady opened the door, removed her apron, fixed her hair and walked out to the car. She had a beautiful warm smile.

"Hi, I'm Andre's mother," she said as Franjo rolled down the window. "Andre is just getting ready. He'll be out in a few minutes."

"Pleased to meet you. I'm Franjo, Bozo's father, and this is Bozo. Welcome to Slavlov," said Franjo as he shook her hand.

"Thank you very much," said Andre's mother. "Andre has told me a lot about you, Bozo. He can't stop talking about his new friend," she continued with a beaming smile.

"He's my circus assistant," said Bozo.

"Bozo and I love the Circus. I am from a Circus

family," explained Franjo.

"Ah yes," said Andre's mother, her face becoming a lot more serious. She looked like she wanted to talk about something else.

"Bozo, Franjo, Andre isn't the same as everybody else. He's ... well ... he's em. Well, he isn't as fast as everyone else".

Bozo wasn't surprised by what Andre's mother had said. He was just surprised that she had said it to him. Comments like that were usually for adults and not children.

"He's great. Andre is wonderful and he is such a great friend and great magician, but he isn't as clever as everybody else and he needs you to look out for him. Bozo, will you promise me you will look out for Andre?" she asked.

Bozo already had a sense that he would have to

look out for Andre, but he also knew that Andre and Oscar would look out for him, so he didn't mind.

"Yes, ma'am. Andre is my best friend and that's what best friends do," he said with a smile.

"Thanks. His father used to protect him but he was killed in the war a few months ago, and now it's just us and we're new here and I worry about him," she said, still sad and looking concerned.

"Hello, Bozo. Hello, Mr. Bozo," said Andre as he raced out of the caravan into the back seat, with Oscar on his shoulder.

"Hello, Andre and Oscar. Great to see you," they both replied overenthusiastically, to reassure his mother.

"Okay, Mom, gotta go. We've got some work to do," said Andre as they drove off and down into Port Alexandrov.

Meet Mr. Edwards

Bozo and Andre talked excitedly about the circus show on Friday night. After a while Bozo noticed that his father was very quiet.

"Why are you so sad?" asked Bozo.

"I don't know, son," replied Franjo.

"Is it because of Friday?" Bozo was worried that his dad was getting cold feet about the show on Friday night.

"Umm," he responded.

Bozo had no idea if that was a yes or a no. "I know Mom really doesn't want us to do this show on Friday but we have to do it, Dad."

"I know ... but I'll change her mind," he said

with a knowing smile.

“Oh, look at that. That must be Mr. Edwards’ yacht.” Franjo pointed to the largest yacht on the port.

“Whose yacht?” asked Bozo

“Mr. Edwards - the man I told you about that can make anyone a star,” said Franjo.

“He certainly has a massive yacht.”

“I know. Some of the local crew were talking about it during the week. It’s one of the biggest in the world. It has a swimming pool, a Jacuzzi, three bars, four sitting rooms, two helicopter pads, a cinema, a dance floor and a staff of over thirty servants.”

“Wow!” Bozo couldn’t believe that someone could own something so big.

“And that’s only his holiday home. Lucky guy!”

This is the man that is going to make me and my father famous circus stars, thought Bozo as if it was a certainty.

"I'm going to get Mr. Edwards to come to see us," piped up Bozo.

Franjo rubbed Bozo on the head. "You really don't live in the real world."

"Yes I do. Look, there's his yacht."

"Bozo, stay away from the yacht. You know the rules; we have to stick to the yachts that we are paid to clean, okay?" said Franjo.

"Okay?" he asked again.

"Ummm," replied Bozo.

"I mean it, Bozo. If you go over there we'll get fired and this is our only income. If we lose it, Bozo, we will have no money - nothing."

Franjo and Bozo pulled up to the harbour and parked their truck, which looked very rusty. Some of the residents of the yachts poked their heads out to see what the noise was and they were very unimpressed to see this rusty machine, an eyesore in their picture-perfect peaceful setting.

The summer was over and the season was winding down. Tonight was the last night Franjo and Bozo would be working on the yacht. Their duties were simple. Polish the rosewood floor and make the brass on the railings, bar, bell and anything else, shine. Make it sparkle.

The golden rule for any member of staff when working on the yachts was to absolutely never to repeat to anyone what they saw on board.

They were also not allowed to talk to the clients.

They were simply there to do a job. Bozo's father taught him the principle of the three wise monkeys: hear no evil, see no evil and speak no evil. It was a rule that Franjo was very strict about.

Bozo couldn't face going into school the next morning. Nor could he face going home to see his parents and grandmother fight again over money or jobs or people looking down on them because they were poor. He knew his father would be mad with him and make things worse but he just had to do something. And so he sneaked out of the yacht and ran as fast as he could in the dark, along the stone walls, keeping away from the lamp lights so no one could see him, and soon he was moments away from the stairs up to Mr. Edwards' yacht.

Bozo admired the flowers on the deck and the amazing gold and silver table setting. In the background, a violinist and pianist played softly.

He heard Mr. Edwards say to one of his staff:

"So, when Sandy sits down, you bring the cushion for me to kneel on. Bring the ring and, when I ask, 'Will you marry me?' and she says 'Yes', nod to the skipper who will signal a beam of light across the harbour, where the engineer will set off the fireworks that spell out 'I love you, Sandy'. Perfect. This is going to be the best night of my life," said Mr. Edwards excitedly.

Why would anyone want to get married? thought Bozo. *I hate girls.*

"Okay, I'm just popping up to have a shower and get ready. This is going to be so exciting!" Mr. Edwards sang again at the absolute top of his lungs.

Moments later, Sandy swooped down the oak staircase to the deck, wearing a simple elegant red dress, hair curled and make-up perfected. Usually she liked to keep her man waiting, but not tonight. Tonight she was early.

Bozo was transfixed by the gorgeous woman. She looked like a movie star.

"Okay, maybe I'd marry *her*, but that's it," he said under his breath, resolute in his dislike for girls.

Sandy was tall and slim, with olive skin, dark eyes and a beaming, broad smile. But her most gorgeous feature was her long, thick, curly hair.

Bozo could see that Mr. Edwards was busy tonight but this was his one opportunity to get Mr. Edwards to make them into circus superstars. And so, looking left and right, Bozo walked back three steps to jump on board.

“Not so fast!” Bozo felt the hood on his sweater being pulled back as he was about to step on board to talk to Mr. Edwards. He lost his footing.

“Where are you off to?” asked the security man.

Bozo said the first thing he could think of. “I’m working on Mr. Edwards yacht I’m here to polish his rosewood floors."

The security man frowned, making it clear that he didn't believe him.

Uh oh, I am in BIG TROUBLE, thought Bozo, who realised he was about to be fired.

The security man lifted him up by the neck of his sweater so that his feet were dangling off the floor.

"Please don't fire me," pleaded Bozo. "I'm here to see Mr. Edwards. I need to speak to him. We have no money and I hate school and I've no friends and my dad - he's the king of the circus - and if I could just ..."

"Get out of here fast," said the man, his nose almost touching Bozo's.

"Put the boy down," roared a man from the deck of the yacht.

"You okay, son?"

"He wants to meet you, sir. He thinks you can make him a star," said the security man, sneering at Bozo.

"What's so wrong with that? If the boy wants to be a star badly enough to risk getting beaten up by you, he must be good. Come on board, son" replied Mr. Edwards.

Bozo jumped onto deck and Mr. Edwards pulled up a fancy chair for him to sit on.

"Now tell me son, what's your name?" asked Mr. Edwards.

"It's Bozo, sir" replied Bozo.

"What age are you?" asked Mr. Edwards.

"I'm nine and a half, sir," replied Bozo. Mr. Edwards smiled and patted him on the head.

"Nice to meet you Bozo. My name is Zeljko and

I'm seventy-five and a half but most people know me as Chuck Edwards since I moved to America," said Mr. Edwards as he took his pipe out of his pocket and started to smoke it.

"Nice to meet you, Mr. Edwards," said Bozo.

"You know, son, when I was your age my mother and I left this country because we were so poor we couldn't even afford a new pair of shoes. We arrived in New York City and lived on the streets until my mother died that winter from the cold. I lived in an orphanage until I was eighteen and dreamed of being a star too. Only I was such a bad singer my friends were convinced I would put the crows in the trees out of business.

Anyway, I learned to love other people singing and dancing and I know how to spot a star. So now I'm the superstar of making superstars. So show us what you got son," said Mr. Edwards.

"Here?" Bozo asked standing on the deck with no music, no Andre his assistant and no Franjo.

"Hey, a star will shine brightly anywhere! Let's see it," he replied.

Bozo had never performed in front of a stranger before, nor had he performed without his father.

But at that moment he closed his eyes and raised his arms straight over his head. He imagined himself in the world's largest circus ring, with thousands of people chanting his name. Clapping his hands, he created a beat that Mr. Edwards continued for him by clapping as Bozo flipped his legs so high into the sky that he somersaulted 360 degrees, flipping his body into sky and landing on his feet again. Mr. Edwards cheered with every turn. He then jumped into the sky and his legs split 180 degrees in a perfect line. With his next jump his legs were kept perfectly together and in mid-air he tipped his toes with his fingers.

“Bravo, bravo!” cheered Mr. Edwards.

“Bozo! Where are you, Bozo?” he heard his father calling him in the distance.

“That’s my dad. I have to go,” said Bozo breaking his performance and needing to rush off before his father found out where he was.

“There’s more where that came from,” shouted Bozo as he was leaving the yacht. “Come to the circus tent on the top of the mountain, Friday night at eight. Me and my father, or my father and I, we’ll be there. He’s the Circus King and

I'm the prince".

Mr. Edwards laughed. "I'd be honoured your highness," he said as he bowed and laughed a hearty laugh.

Go Get 'Em

There was something special about the Friday night circus show. Bozo felt it as he, his grandmother, mother, and father locked the door of their small cottage and piled into Grandmother's good car.

It was a sunny evening and all the chores of the house had been completed. Everybody was giddy with nervousness. Even Grandmother, who had forgotten about how silly the circus was, wished them both well.

"Do your best," she said with kindness. "That's all you can do. And, my dearest Bozo, you are going to steal the show with your big puppy dog eyes and beautiful smile," she said as she pinched his checks affectionately. He hated that, but he was so excited that he didn't even mind.

His mother was in a white leotard with sliver sequins that glistened against the evening sun as they drove to the circus tent. Her headpiece, which she carefully rested on the floor of the car between her feet, held two enormous white feathers. It would stand proudly on her pretty head. He hair was long and curly and her make-up strong but exquisite. They didn't have the money to buy new costumes, so they used any fabric they could find - curtains, bed sheets, even the sequins were cut from Marija's wedding dress. On this particular evening, Marija and Franjo looked, walked and talked like superstars, and everybody took note.

Walking into the back of the circus, Andre and Oscar were there as promised.

"Thanks for coming, Andre," said Bozo. Oscar tweeted loudly. "You too, Oscar," Bozo added with a laugh. "I need you to be my assistant for the evening. You will need to help me to carry all these large boxes for the tigers, and these hoops for the fire eaters. And you will have to put a towel around my shoulders after my act with my father," he explained, taking charge.

"Why will you need a towel over your shoulders?" Andre asked, as though it was a perfectly logical question.

"Because we're stars and that's what all the stars do," said Bozo. This boy had a lot to learn about show business. "We're in show business now, Andre. Things are different. Things are magical." He beamed excitedly.

"Cool," said Andre as they walked into the ring to prepare for the show.

That night was magical. Seeing Franjo and Bozo perform together was a sight that everyone from around the surrounding villages couldn't wait to witness. This was Franjo's comeback show and many of his old circus friends where there to support him. They were the easiest to spot. They had the loudest voices and the most colourful clothes in the tent. Unfortunately, Grandmother had to sit in front of them and she spent the entire evening turning around and shushing them.

Bozo, Andre and Oscar peered through a hole in the tent to see just how many people had come. There were hundreds.

"Are you nervous?" asked Andre.

"No," Bozo lied.

"I would be," Andre admitted.

"Maybe a little, then," said Bozo, whose nerves had subsided when he saw Mr. Edwards and Sandy shuffling along the front row to their seats beside Grandmother.

"Don't sit there," Bozo pleaded quietly.

"What's wrong?" asked Andre

"There's Mr. Edwards, the man who's going to make us stars, and he's sitting next to my grandmother. He's going to start singing and they'll fight, and he'll leave and then we won't go to America and get away from all this."

"Not to make you more nervous, but that's the least of your worries," said Andre, pointing towards the three members of the Mafia seated in the front row opposite Grandmother, Mr. Edwards and Sandy.

“Oh no! Who let them in?” said Bozo in a panic. “Why are they here? They always said they hated the circus. Can’t they just leave me alone?” Wasn’t it enough that they terrorised him in school? Now they were going to ruin his chance to get away from them.

“Okay, change of plan, you two,” said Bozo, who was beginning not to see Oscar as an imaginary friend anymore. In fact, he was beginning to see the three of them as a team. “Forget about all the things I asked you to do earlier on. Your job tonight is to keep an eye on those three and make sure that they don’t ruin anything for me,” he commanded.

Just a few seconds before they went on stage, Bozo, Andre and Oscar looked over to Marija and Franjo.

"You are the most beautiful woman in the world, Marija, and I love you with every beat of my heart. If the last ten years were a taste of what is to come for us both, then I want to do it over and over and over again," Franjo said.

Not wanting to smudge her make-up, Marija took his hands as the audience's applause swelled in anticipation of the start of the show.

"You are the most handsome man I have ever seen and I love you more and more each day," she replied.

"Well, that's embarrassing," Andre told Bozo, who blushed for his parents.

"Tell me about it," said Bozo, as he lowered his

head in embarrassment.

“You are my sunshine, my only sunshine. You make me happy when skies are grey,” Marija and Franjo sang to each other as they waltzed arm in arm, oblivious to anyone looking on.

“Mooom,” Bozo whined. “Not in front of everyone, please”

Marija and Franjo laughed. “Oh Bozo, you’ll be like this, too, when you get married.”

“Get married?” said Andre and Bozo together. “Why would anyone want to get married to a *girl?*” They choked as though *girl* was the dirtiest word in the world. They both shook their heads in confusion as they turned back to look through the holes at the Mafia and Mr. Edwards.

Grown-up Stuff

Bozo kept his video recorder with him for the entire night to make sure that if the Mafia were going to spoil his night he'd have video evidence.

Walking behind the circus ring, he could hear the faint noise of fighting. It was Sandy. She looked to be arguing with a man who was holding her wrist very tightly and she was trying to make him let go.

Intrigued, he turned on his video recorder to find out what they were saying. The recorder caught everything very clearly.

"I hate seeing you with that man," the young

man whispered. The annoyance in his voice made it louder than he'd intended, causing some passers-by to turn their heads to see the source of the commotion.

Sandy stared at the locals, worried that they'd overheard something. "Oh, he's such a flirt," she said about the man holding her wrist, talking to her. She played with her long diamond earrings and looked away, but she hadn't convinced Bozo. He was all ears.

"Keep your voice down," she snarled at the young man who refused to back off.

"You are my wife! Stop being so friendly to him," he replied.

They're married? thought Bozo.

"In case you hadn't noticed, I'm acting!" said Sandy sarcastically.

"Let's stop this now," the man said desperately. "We can leave tonight and go back to the island."

"No. If we are going to go to war then we need guns and knives and trucks for the soldiers. Where are we going to get the money for this? Mr. Edwards is rich enough for us to win this war. We are not giving up now," said Sandy.

War? What war? Bozo was confused as he recorded the conversation on his video recorder.

"The money will be out of Mr. Edwards' account tomorrow and then we are free," Sandy continued.

Bozo wondered what war they were talking about but he felt sorry for Mr. Edwards, who was obviously being taken for a fool.

We're on Our Way

Even though the Mafia tried the whole night to spoil Franjo and Bozo's acts, Andre and Oscar made sure that didn't happen. Grandmother spent the evening telling Franjo's circus friends to quieten down and she kept nudging Mr. Edwards to stop singing and laughing and cheering so loudly at everything. But Mr. Edwards couldn't help it. He was mesmerised by the magic and the acrobats and the music and, most of all, the talents of Franjo and Bozo. They made it all look so simple that the audience stood and applauded rapturously after every act.

When the performance was over, Sandy trailed behind Mr. Edwards as he elbowed his way past the line of supporters to meet Franjo and Bozo. "Mr. Fantastico Franjo!" Mr. Edwards shook his hand so furiously with excitement that Franjo's hand practically went white from the loss of blood. "I want the whole world to be entertained by you and your magnificent son. I am going to make you an international star. You are going to be rich beyond your wildest dreams."

That night, Bozo was too excited to sleep. Mr. Edwards was going to make him a circus superstar. He had always known it would happen. He just knew that justice would prevail, that the terror in school and the poverty at home were just practice for bigger and better things. It all made sense to him now. If he had had a privileged life, becoming rich and famous and entertaining millions of people would have meant nothing to him. He had experienced tough times, but it was all in preparation for this. The memories of the life that he had lived would keep him and his family working hard to entertain people. But above all, he knew that he would never forget people who had less than he did and would always help them when he was famous.

He knew that his Grandmother would be happy because they would have money and the village would talk about them as a gifted family.

Father would be doing what he had always wanted to do. Mother would be happy because her husband and mother would be happy and she'd have nice clothes and clean hands and would always be pretty. Andre and Oscar would be happy because people would talk to them and like them. And Bozo would get away from the Mafia.

Bozo had it all sorted. After he had resolved that everyone was going to be just fine, he could close his eyes and sleep peacefully.

The next morning was met with hurried excitement and laughter. All of the family's belongings had been packed and they bundled into a chauffeur-driven car to drive to Mr. Edwards's yacht, where they were to meet him at eleven sharp. Andre, his mother and Oscar were to be collected separately and they would all meet up at the airport.

Grandmother could not stop talking during the drive. "I always knew you were going to be famous, Franjo. I could see it all those years ago when Marija and I first set eyes on you the moment you walked into the circus ring," she said. She had apparently forgotten crying for weeks when her well-spoken, highly educated, musically accomplished daughter married the illiterate, unsophisticated performer from a gypsy family.

"Oh, come on, Mother! No you didn't!" said Marija playfully. She didn't often stand up to her mother, but there was an atmosphere of fun and cheeky confidence on this very special day amongst the whole family.

"Yes, I did, dear," said Grandmother.

"Well, if you did, then I saw it first," said Marija as she lovingly combed her fingers through Franjo's hair. "I saw it so much that I married it," she said proudly.

"And don't we all deserve this success?" said Franjo, ever the peacemaker.

"We'll be the talk of the village," said Grandmother proudly. "They'll all want to know us now. It's all in the rearing," she said, congratulating herself, with a smile.

"Oh, come on!" said Marija, Franjo and Bozo in unison. All four of them shared a hearty laugh. Their driver pulled up at the entrance to Mr. Edwards's yacht. The chauffeur got out of the front seat and opened the door to let them out. "Thank you," said Franjo, Marija and Bozo one by one as they excitedly jumped out of the car and made their way up the ramp.

"My suitcase is the pink one and it has some very delicate items, so please do be careful with it," said Grandmother, leaving the car last.

"Of course, ma'am," said the driver.

"I expect two sausages and two fried eggs - soft - in the morning, or 'sunny side up' as they say in America," she continued, unaware that you don't give your breakfast order to the driver.

"That's no problem, ma'am," said the driver, too polite to point this out.

"And also, please make sure that there is no dust in the car in future. I have bad asthma and it doesn't help when I'm travelling."

Grandmother had entered the world of celebrity with ease.

"That's no problem, ma'am."

They boarded the yacht, following Bozo, who knew his way around. The first thing they saw was an amazing view of the blue seas and the clear skies that made Vladislav look every bit a paradise destination.

Bozo continued looking around for Mr. Edwards, but he was nowhere to be seen.

"Mr. Edwards!" called Bozo. "Mr. Edwards?" He raised his voice just a little, not wanting to be disrespectful, but they heard no response, just the faint sounds of ... well, they weren't quite sure.

They followed the noise through the dining room, onto balcony and then up the stairs to the helipad. Mr. Edwards was sitting with his head in his hands, sobbing with all of his heart.

"Mr. Edwards, what is it? What's wrong?" they all asked as they rushed to console him.

"She's left me," was the only sentence they could understand between the sobs.

"Who's left you?" asked Bozo.

"Sandy left me ... and she's taken lots of my money!" he cried.

"What?"

They all sat frozen in disbelief, heartbroken for Mr. Edwards.

"I am so sorry," he said, lifting his head, his big, bulging eyes red and raw from crying. "I am so sorry, but we can't go to America - not today. I'm too sad."

There was a long silence. Each member of the family felt a twinge of sorrow, but nobody had the bad manners to express it. Not even Bozo, who was devastated.

"Don't worry, Mr. Edwards. I'm sure the police will find Sandy soon enough and you will get your money back," said Marija, her kind heart always winning out over selfishness. "You can stay with us in the meantime. It's a small house, but it's lots of fun and there's plenty to do. Let us be your family for a little while."

"Thank you," he grabbed Marija's hand tightly. His memories of being orphaned still haunted him, even as a seventy-five-year-old man.

Bozo and his family travelled back to Bozo's house in silence. Only a few hours ago, the whole future made sense. Now nothing did, and Bozo was too disappointed to figure it out.

Ah Well

Everyone was feeling a little sorry for themselves. The silence in the house was eerie. But they were too busy pining about what would have been to notice.

The ever-emotional Mr. Edwards was the worst. Sandy was the only woman he'd ever loved and, up until that day, he had been convinced she'd been worth the wait. He had loved her with every beat of his heart. He wondered how he could have been such a fool.

Everyone consoled him with the clichés: you weren't to know, she fooled everyone; she won't have any luck for it. This consoled him a little, but deep down this seventy-five-year-old man was still a sad young orphan. The unspoken reason he felt foolish was that deep down he'd always know she would leave him. Maybe that was the reason he had never opened his heart before. And hadn't he been right? He had everything in life apart from the one thing that mattered to him the most: to be part of a family. It wasn't often that Mr. Edwards felt sorry for himself, or had a frown on his face, but today he gave himself full permission to be miserable.

Across the room in the usual spot under the shade of the apple trees, Grandmother sat with her face in her hands. "What will the villagers say when they see we haven't left?" she said out loud. "Of course they'll be sympathetic when I explain, but once my back is turned the gossiping will start".

Bozo knew that she felt rather silly at how she'd bragged about their journey to fame and fortune but he knew there would be a few people who would delight in her misfortune.

Marija wanted a better life for Bozo. Bozo wanted a better life for himself. He also wondered if he could have stopped Sandy and warned Mr. Edwards. It was too late now, but maybe if he had said something they would be sailing to America.

"What do you look so grumpy for?"

Grandmother asked Mr. Edwards in an unusually aggressive tone. She usually saved her insults until after her guests had departed. "Mother!" exclaimed Marija, who was usually the one being corrected for her lack of social etiquette.

"Why do you think?" snapped Mr. Edwards. "She was too young for you anyway," said Grandmother matter-of-factly.

"I beg your pardon" asked Mr. Edwards, He had been living in such a free world that he hadn't considered something so old fashioned in years. He was too powerful for people to mention it or for him to listen.

"You should be acting your age. The two of you looked ridiculous together and everyone was laughing at you. Of course she was only after your money. You're seventy-five, for heaven's sake. Did you honestly think she was going to stick with you forever?" Grandmother continued, seeming annoyed that *she* had to point out the obvious.

Normally Mr. Edwards was a man oblivious to the social norm of holding emotions in, but because of Grandmother's hurtful comments, he did his best to hold back and preserve his dignity.

"You have more money than you could ever spend. Life has been very kind to you, Mr. Edwards, and you should be grateful," said Grandmother, put off by Mr. Edwards's self-pity. "Look at the people of Slavlov. None of us here have been able to afford a holiday in our lives. We can't afford to furnish or paint the house. Marija and Franjo have been saving all year for a bike for Bozo's tenth birthday". "You got me a bike?" Bozo brightened at the news.

"It was supposed to be a surprise," said Marija starting at Grandmother.

"Money is not my yardstick for happiness" said Mr. Edwards firmly. "I may have all the money in the world but you have each other. If it wasn't for the kindness of Marija here, I would be sitting in that big boat on my own, alone again. But you have each other. And I know you think your house is too small, and your car needs to be replaced, and your clothes could be nicer. But believe me, you are richer than me and your wealth has given you more happiness than mine ever could."

Mr. Edwards had silenced the room. They all, part from Franjo, saw their blessings in a different light for the first time. Franjo, for his part, had always known this. There was an awkward silence as everyone stared at the floor or out the window.

"Did you really save all year, Mother" asked Bozo, delighted with the prospect of a new bike, but guilty they'd had to save for so long with his birthday still weeks away.

"Yes, Bozo, and we'd do it again every year if it meant making you happy," said Marija, putting her hands on his shoulders and finishing her sentence with a kiss to his forehead.

Franjo thought that with the big disappointment of the day, Bozo could use something to cheer him up. He went out to the back of the shed and rang the bell on Bozo's bike as he cycled over to the half door of the kitchen. Bozo couldn't contain his excitement. Franjo swung open the door and cycled in on a two-foot-tall bike, not even big enough for a four year old. Bozo was horrified.

"Dad?" He was in so much shock he couldn't get his thoughts together.

"What's wrong?" Franjo asked, looking genuinely surprised by the reaction.

"It's tiny," said Bozo. "Everyone's going to laugh at me when they see me cycling that."

Marija, Mr. Edwards and Grandmother were stunned.

"Can you not get anything right?" snapped Grandmother. Nobody came to Franjo's defense.

"Look, if it's too small, you can adjust the saddle." Franjo extended the saddle to meet his waist, which made the bike looks even more ridiculous.

"We saved all year for *that*?" Marija looked ready to burst into tears.

“It’s okay, Mother. I really like it. Thank you,” said Bozo, trying unsuccessfully to pretend to be happy.

“Aaaah.... I’m only joking!” said Franjo. He swiftly went back into the yard and brought in a large blue mountain bike with twenty gears, razor-sharp brakes and multi-coloured reflectors. It was everything that Bozo had out on his wish list.

Everyone laughed heartily, including Mr. Edwards, who laughed the longest and the hardest.

“Mr. Edwards, you are part of our family now,” said Franjo in an uplifting tone. “Let’s go outside and do some fishing.”

That evening, Bozo spent hours on his early birthday present. He decided to pay his father a visit by the lake.

"Are you not sad, Father?" he asked, sitting down beside him in the peaceful setting. Franjo hadn't shown any emotion since they had returned from Mr. Edward's yacht. "Sad?" said Franjo with a smile. "I couldn't be happier. You and your mother, and even your Grandmother," he whispered, "are the most important things in the world to me. I don't need to be famous to know that. I love being in the circus, but for nothing other than the freedom and enjoyment I give to people. If we were meant to set sail on that yacht today, Bozo, we would have. But we didn't. I didn't have a family when I was a young boy and that made me very sad. Today I have a family and that is the most important thing, isn't it?" Bozo barely nodded his head. He knew what his father was saying was true, but he was still very disappointed he didn't get to go to America. "Now what's so bad about Slavlov?" Franjo asked.

"I hate school," Bozo answered, not needing much more probing.

"Bozo, from this day forth you are to be fearless. We are all meant to shine. So you can set an example in your class, okay? Slavlov is not America, but who cares? When you're a star, you'll shine anywhere you are. And maybe, just for now, you are meant to shine in Slavlov. Be fearless and afraid of nobody. You don't need a seventy-five-year-old man to tell you that, do you?" he asked. "You don't need a bank account full of money to make you believe that, do you?"

Bozo shook his head. His father always made him feel better.

"Of course not. Now let's start enjoying life" said Franjo. Bozo was beginning to feel a lot better.

Bozo and Franjo spent the evening happily entertaining Marija, Grandmother and Mr. Edwards in the summer evening sun. No one complained. Mr. Edwards spent hours retelling stories of the magical world of entertainment, which someday Bozo still hoped to be part of.

Not the Dream I Meant

The day had been a roller coaster of emotions and everyone thought it best to head to bed early. For the first time in weeks, Bozo's excitement had subsided and he slept heavily. He awoke to the sound of a thundering bang on the front door of their cottage. Jumping out of his bed, grabbing his video recorder, he heard the sound of grown men shouting in the kitchen. Their voices bellowed around the house. Bozo's heart pounded so badly that his throat start to get tight. He was completely frozen with fear. Suddenly the door burst open as Grandmother charged into the room and put her hand tightly over Bozo's mouth, dragging him over to the big old dresser beside his bed. She pushed and pushed until the dresser inched forward to reveal a secret passage into a dark room. In all of Bozo's years of exploring and playing he had never found this passage. Still holding Bozo's mouth, Grandmother carried him into the dark musty room. Holding his grandmothers' hand very tightly, Bozo walked down the wooden stairway in complete darkness. The sound of angry voices grew louder and louder. Bozo feared for the rest of his family and Mr. Edwards. He hoped there was another bunker on the other side of the house. In that moment, Bozo pulled his hand out of his grandmother's grasp and ran back up the stairs towards the trap door to save them. But grandmother caught him by his shins and pulled him back down.

"But Granny, where's Mother?" he asked.

"Shush," she whispered into Bozo's ear, "stay here, Bozo. You have to stay here and be very quiet. Otherwise the soldiers will kill us."

"Soldiers? Kill us?" said Bozo. "Kill us?" he repeated. He was terrified.

Grandmother and Bozo huddled into the corner of the dark bunker. Above them faint rays of moonlight shone through the decayed parts of the wooden floorboards. They could just about see the soldiers in the yard. They could also hear the faint screams of locals being tortured nearby. Huddled with his grandmother in terror, Bozo realized that this wasn't just happening to his family. It was happening to the whole village. The torture continued as they heard the screams of Franjo and Mr. Edwards being beaten by the soldiers. Suddenly the trap door burst open and for a split second their hearts stopped beating in anticipation of a brutal killer coming to murder them. Thankfully it was Marija, who had been able to make it to the bunker safely. Forgetting grandmother's strict instructions to remain still, Bozo could not control his relief and ran up the stairs to embrace his mother.

"Bozo, come back," said grandmother in a loud firm whisper. This time she had been too slow to catch him as he shot up the stairs. As Bozo and his mother hugged, they again heard the screams of his father and Mr. Edwards being beaten outside.

Fearless, thought Bozo, *Fearless and afraid of no one*, he repeated to himself as he pushed open the door, pulled the dresser away and ran through his bedroom and into the yard. His mother and grandmother screamed “Bozo, come back!” they yelled as they watched him run towards danger.

Fearless and afraid of no one, Bozo ran into the yard and saw his father, who lay on the ground beaten, bloody and weak. Beside him, a young solider beat him with the end of his rifle over and over again. He kicked him, punched him and smashed his face.

Bozo knew the dangerous ground he was treading on, but he could not watch the soldiers kill his father. Even at nine years old, Bozo knew that he would never forgive himself if he did not fight for his father. Bozo ran up behind the solider. With all of his energy, he jumped on the soldier's back and beat him with his fists.

"Leave my father alone, you monster," he yelled. "Leave him alone, you pig!"

"Bozo, nooooo," he heard his father's faint plea, as the fierce man turned around and hit Bozo so hard on his face that he was hurled into the air. His face bled uncontrollably as his head hit the hard ground and knocked him unconscious.

Hell

Bozo opened his eyes very slowly. They stung so badly that they almost refused to open. He had to pull them apart with his fingers. For a few moments he was totally disoriented.

Where am I? he thought in his dozy state, with just a vague memory of his house being attacked. Bozo looked around, his eyes searching for the familiar wallpaper in his bedroom. He even hoped that today he would have to go to school.

He blinked again and licked his lips slowly, as they also stung with the pain of his swollen face. He lifted his hand to cradle his sore mouth, slowly making sense of what had happened to him. His heart sank when he realised that night was not a bad dream. In front of him, he could see a green galvanised wall and the cold, steel, dirty floor of an army truck. Lifting his head, he saw a row of five boys hunkered down, cradling themselves in shock. Their faces were so sad. Bozo was beginning to piece together the horror of what had happened to his family, and to his entire village.

A stern-faced solider sat at the end of the truck holding a long rifle. He was wearing an army uniform: green trousers; big, dirty, black boots; green beret on his head; green camouflage shirt; and a stern, cold face. He shouted at Bozo. “Oh, I see the prince has woken,” he mocked. “You are a prince, I hear. A circus prince,” he laughed.

“Where is your king?” he continued, revealing his crooked, filthy teeth. “Well, your royal highness, let’s see your magic and watch you disappear from here!”

Bozo avoided his piercing, angry gaze as he stared at the floor, humiliated. No one else was laughing.

“Let’s see it,” the soldier shouted again, pushing his nose up against Bozo’s face. “Well, let’s see it.” He pulled Bozo up by the neck of his shirt, lifted him up against the wall and roared into his face.

Bozo fought back tears. “I am not a magician, sir. I am a circus performer.” Bozo had just about used up all his bravery for one day.

"Is there a difference? You fool! You and your family." He paced up and down the truck.

"And, you, what's your name?" The soldier pointed to the sobbing boy beside Bozo. Bozo looked around and there he was, the tough man himself, crying his heart out: Vito, leader of the Mafia, reduced to tears by this terrifying soldier.

"Vito, sir," the boy answered sheepishly.

"My name is Dalibor, meaning to fight, and that is what we are here to do. Enough," said Dalibor as he slammed on the steel floor, indicating to the driver that he should leave. "Enough, I said. Let's get out of this dump." With that instruction, the soldier in the front seat of the truck drove through the village of Slavlov.

Sitting across from Bozo, rocking on his hunkers, was Andre. Oscar was hidden under his jumper. Andre shook with fear. Rocking on his own, hugging Oscar, he whispered, “I can’t find my mammy. I can’t find her.”

“I can’t find my family either, Andre,” said Bozo.

He had run out of bravery, and fearlessness and hopeful things to say. Today he was not a protector. And today, more than any day, Bozo needed to be protected.

The truck drove through the sandy roads of Slavlov. Bozo and the boys looked at the devastation that had hit the village. But even seeing the burnt-out school and bombed buildings, all Bozo felt was total numbness. No emotion, no fear, no grief, not even belief.

Bozo knew that this was worse than the most tragic of his father's stories. This was the darkest day of his life. He knew that nothing else could happen that would be worse, yet still all he felt was utter numbness. The truck passed by his cottage and he watched the last wooden beams of his small but perfect home go up in flames. All he and his family owned was gone, and he had no idea where his family were or even if they were still alive.

As the truck exited the village, the ten boys sat in silence. They were shocked and afraid. The smell in the truck was so unbearable that every so often Bozo's stomach heaved with the stench. The smell of sweat and dirt from the army men was disgusting. The boys were in deep thought, reflecting and trying to make sense of the horror they had witnessed.

At home Bozo's family had often discussed whether hell existed and where it was and what it looked like. Was it underground, with fire and men wearing horns and dragons and no sunshine or singing or circus tricks? He'd always thought that that you had to die before you found out where hell was. Bozo didn't know if hell was a place. If it was on a map. If it was under the ground or behind a rainbow. But that day knew that hell was a feeling, a feeling beyond terror and fear and nervousness. Bozo knew that buildings could be rebuilt, that the rain would stop, that the sun would rise in the morning and that somehow life would go on. But hell was a feeling of nothingness and no hope. Hell was the coldness he had seen. Hell was the anger that these men had inside them. Bozo realised just then what hell really was. He had lost every member of his family and his village. Bozo could think of nothing worse.

Staying Alive

The noise of the truck's engine had lulled each of the boys to sleep. They had driven through the mountains for hours. Bozo woke to the sudden sound of silence when the engine was switched off.

"Okay, you rats," shouted the soldier, again pacing up and down the truck, you are here to do your duty," he yelled, reaching down to unbuckle the big, dirty suitcase that lay on the floor.

What duty? thought Bozo, who had absolutely no comprehension of why their families were being punished. He dreaded what was coming next, but he dared not ask.

"Tweet!" Oscar was a little braver, but it couldn't have come at a worse time.

"What was that noise?" said the solider, frowning as he looked at Andre.

"What noise?" asked timid Andre, who may as well have put his hand up and said "I'm guilty," by responding to the question at all.

Bozo sat holding his breath, hoping Oscar would stay quiet and the solider would find someone else to pick on, namely Vito.

"Tweet," Oscar called from the comfort of Andre's top pocket, under his jumper.

"Is that a ... a ... a ... *bird?*" the soldier asked.

"No," said Andre, who was visibly blushing and panicking. It was the first time that Bozo had ever seen him lie. And that was for a good reason: he was no good at it. But he had lost absolutely everything in his life and he simply could not live without Oscar.

"It's Andre and his stupid bird," said Vito, pointing to Andre as if no one knew. Bozo was disgusted. Even though they were all going to die, and he knew that Andre loved Oscar, he was still causing trouble. What difference would it have made to him whether Oscar was there or not? Bozo was beginning to think that not only were they in hell, but the Devil was sitting beside him.

"Oh, it must be a singing jumper, then," said the solider as he tore open Andre's jumper and ripped Oscar out of his shirt pocket. He held the tiny bird in his massive, grubby, hands.

"We *especially* don't like birds," said the

solider, rubbing Oscar with his dirty paws. “That is why we are going to kill it.” He stared at Andre, almost delighted at the thought of inflicting more terror on the poor boy.

“Don’t kill him,” shouted Bozo, who had forgotten about his empty fuel tank of bravery and needed to stand up for his friend.

Slowly the solider placed his hand over his other hand to cup Oscar and break his neck, but at the last moment Andre stamped on the soldier’s foot and Oscar flew away.

“Noooooo!” shouted Andre. “Daddy, come back. Come back, Daddy. Don’t leave me, Daddy. Please don’t leave me.” Andre tried to run after Oscar, but the solider grabbed him. This was just more ammunition for the sarcastic comments of this filthy man.

"Daddy? Your daddy's a bird? Are you not a little too old for imaginary friends?" he asked sneeringly.

"He's not an imag ... an imag ... an ..." stuttered Andre.

"Oh, poor little boy, can't say the big word," said the soldier.

"He's not an imaginary friend. He's our friend," piped up Bozo, who had nothing to lose and couldn't bear to watch his friend suffer any more.

"Don't worry, Andre, he'll come back and find us," said Bozo bravely in front of the boys and Dalibor.

"Aren't you all a little too old for make believe?" Dalibor asked. "Well, this is not make believe. This is real life. We are at war and you will be our defenders."

He bent down again and opened the large leather case to reveal ten rifles, one for each boy.

"Tonight you will surround the city and you will kill. Do you hear me? You will kill," he ordered.

Bozo was shocked. He had resigned himself to his own death, but he knew that to take the life of another was wrong. It was just wrong and Bozo could not do it.

"If you die, you die. There is nothing to live for anyway. Your families are all dead," he shouted.

Your families are dead. That sentence went through Bozo's mind in slow motion over and over.

Are they all dead? Is this just another of this

man's jokes? he wondered, trying to comprehend it. He watched as all the boys, one by one, reacted to the same piece of information. They cried silently, burying their heads in their hands.

The solider continued to show the boys how to use a rifle but it was background noise as they each came to terms with this horrific reality.

Be Careful

Later that night the boys were given a tray of cold soup and hard bread.

"After you have eaten, you will get some sleep and just before the sun rises we will set to work on fighting the enemy," he commanded.

What enemy? thought Bozo. He didn't know what this was all about or why they were being asked to fight, much less what where they fighting for.

A few hours later the boys slept, still curled up in balls and resting against each other for pillows. Snoring loudly in the corner, holding his rifle, Dalibor guarded the exit.

Bozo couldn't sleep. He carefully looked

through the holes in the galvanised walls to see the forest that surrounded them. Their truck was parked on the top of a hill overlooking a large city full of lights.

In the quiet of the night Bozo looked around to make sure no-one was awake. He very gently removed his video recorder from his top pocket. He smoothed off all the sand from when he had fallen to the ground and checked to see that it was not broken.

Outside he heard the noise of a car coming towards the truck and parking outside. Dalibor woke and Bozo quickly closed his eyes pretending to be asleep.

Dalibor jumped out of the truck and walked over to the car. Bozo opened his eyes again and peered outside. Dalibor stood talking to a man and a woman. They then all walked closer to the truck.

Sandy, thought Bozo. It was Sandy who had come to the truck with the same man whom he had seen her talk to at the circus.

Sandy stood right outside the truck where Bozo was. Bozo very slowly and carefully pressed the record button on his video recorder. He could hear every word very clearly. He knew that he couldn't make a sound.

"Where is the rest of the money?" asked Dalibor as Sandy handed Dalibor a bag of cash.

"The money is almost spent," said Sandy. "We have bought as many trucks and guns and bullets as we can."

"We need more," said Dalibor, "much more."

I know," said Sandy as she turned to walk to the

car. “I am working on it”.

Run

Just before dawn, a golden glow of light passed by Bozo's closed eyes, waking him gently. In front of him was a sight he had witnessed only once before, when he and Andre had agreed to be friends. Oscar was glowing, golden and bright as a light bulb, flapping wildly inside the truck. Looking around, Bozo checked that Dalibor and the other boys were still asleep. They were, apart from Andre, who had just woken excitedly.

"Daddy, you came back to save me," said Andre, who hadn't given up hope.

"Shush," mouthed the smart-thinking Bozo as

he placed his finger over his lips to make sure that Andre didn't wake Dalibor and get them killed.

But Andre was one step ahead. He reached over, using Oscar as his light to see what he was doing, and very gently tied Dalibor's shoelaces together, as the soldier still gripped his gun while sleeping.

Suddenly Oscar flew out of the truck, and Andre raced after him. For a split moment, Bozo considered what to do. If he stayed, he'd have to kill; if he left, he'd be killed. He decided to run for it, past Dalibor and down into the city. But he tripped over Dalibor's feet, waking him from his snores. Not looking back, Andre and Bozo ran through the forest and into the city, following Oscar's golden glow through the narrow, winding footpaths of this unknown city. Behind them, Dalibor had quickly untied his shoelaces and he chased after them, shouting, “Get back here! I demand you get back here,” He fired bullets at their legs. Each time, he just missed his target.

Bozo and Andre ran faster than they had ever run in their lives through the cobbled streets. They could hear Dalibor shooting and they were all too aware that, any minute, their lives could be over.

The bullets hit the stone walls of the city as Dalibor gained speed and closed in on them. The other two soldiers from the front of the truck had been woken by the commotion and were running behind Dalibor. But Andre and Oscar ran with their eyes firmly fixed on golden Oscar, who led the way towards the sea.

They sped through the narrow city streets, zigzagging through bars, shops and markets.

“I can’t run anymore,” said Andre, stopping suddenly when he had run further than he ever thought possible. But Oscar kept flying and they couldn’t afford to lose him.

“Andre, *please,*” begged Bozo. “If we stop, we will die. Please, Andre.” Bozo was begging for his life. He didn’t want to travel this unknown road without his friend. He simply couldn’t.

“Please, Andre, I don’t want to leave you,” he pleaded.

“Go on, Bozo. I just can’t ...” he said, barely able to catch his breath.

“Gotcha, you piece of filthy scum,” yelled the

solider as he put his hand on Andre's shoulder.

"And *you,*" he yelled at Bozo. "You're behind all this, aren't you?" He reached out his arm to grab hold of Bozo. But as he did, for the first time in his life, Bozo used all of his training with his father to his advantage, just like his father had said he would.

As the solider reached his arm out towards him, Bozo jumped three feet into the air and dropkicked the powerhouse of a man onto the ground. His rifle fell and a shot went off. Andre picked it up.

"Don't shoot," commanded Bozo, who was not in familiar territory but knew not to kill.

"Give me the gun, Andre," he said. Andre passed the gun over to him keeping the barrel firmly pointed at Dalibor.

Dalibor rose onto his knees as he began begging. “Don’t shoot me, please don’t shoot me.”

“Are you going to kill us?” asked Bozo, mimicking Dalibor’s earlier tone.

“No ... I won’t, I promise,” he said, weeping as he begged for his life.

“Will you let us go?” asked Andre, who could hear the sound of the other soldiers nearby.

“Yes ... yes ... just don’t shoot me.” This beast of a man had been reduced to tears. Bozo was surprised to see him crumble so easily and weep like a baby.

“You don’t understand,” he continued as the tears flowed. “I was your age when I became a soldier. I was taken from my family, too, seven years ago.”

The boys were stunned, but they needed to get out of there fast.

"Please run. Don't live the life I have lived. Run before the older soldiers find you. With that, Bozo and Andre threw the gun into the sea. They saw the other soldiers running after them, shooting and yelling. In the distance, they saw the faint but distinctive glow of Oscar. In a hail of bullets, they followed him, almost in a trance, towards the docklands and onto an enormous cargo ship whose doors were closing. Safely on the ship, they ran over to a small oval window and looked out at the city as the ship set sail. The soldiers had surrounded Dalibor, who was lying on the ground. They beat him with their rifles in the same way that they had beaten Bozo's father. They paused for a moment. Bloody and beaten, Dalibor rose to his knees and clasped his hands in a begging position. The boys could clearly make out that he was pleading for his life. They knew it was because he had set them free. They continued to peer out of the window, looking at their future had they stayed on that truck any longer. And at sixteen years of age, Dalibor was shot dead on the pavement.

Anywhere But Here

Bozo, Andre and Oscar made a bed for themselves between the massive wooden boxes that held the ship's cargo. After what had happened, none of them wanted to explore the ship to find out where they were going or even if there was anywhere warmer for them to sleep. All they knew was that if they wanted to stay alive, they had to stay where they were until the ship docked. That might be in five hours' time, or in five weeks' time. But they weren't about ask anyone and risk being sent back home.

After all they'd been through, Andre and Bozo

could talk about anything. They were friends and that's what friends do. But tonight neither of them could muster the emotion to talk about what had just happened. Both lay awake silently. They kept replaying the events of the last few days over and over in their minds. It had been the most extraordinary few days - nearly becoming circus superstars; their homes being attacked; being told that their families were dead; and now leaving their country in a hail of bullets with absolutely no idea of where they were going. Bozo cradled his video recorder and batteries in his hands. He could not face looking at the images of home - not just yet. It would make him too sad.

Although Bozo and Andre should have been bored, they weren't. They just talked and looked out the window at the vast seas and the darkening weather. Every so often, in the distance, they could hear the sounds of drunken sailors playing cards, and their hearts would start pounding for fear of being caught. They would stare at Oscar who they now trusted would make sure that they kept out of danger. If Oscar glowed again, it was a sign to follow him out of harm's way.

The drunken noises were becoming more frequent and seemed to be getting a lot closer. Bozo, Andre and Oscar felt it was no longer safe to stay so openly in the cargo hold. If one of these sailors looked around the corner, there was nowhere for the boys to hide. If they were caught, they would be sent home, and that meant being sent to fight, which almost certainly meant death.

One evening they heard the familiar sound of the sailors playing cards and laughing. They would always finish the night with a sing-song, which Bozo, Andre and Oscar sort of enjoyed. That night, however, the sound of one of the men's voices became louder and louder and it sounded like his footsteps were coming closer and closer. The boys stared at Oscar. He glowed a golden hue and very quietly flew to a nearby cargo box. Andre and Bozo crept behind him and stopped right beside one of the many wooden containers. Oscar tapped the cylinder with his beak. Andre knew exactly what to do. Bozo couldn't help thinking that Oscar and Andre had a secret language, and if he wanted to survive, he was going to have to learn it fast.

Andre's hand felt its way along the wooden box, but all sides appeared sealed.

"Where Oscar? I can't find anything," said Andre.

"The boxes are all full of figs, Oscar. We can't go inside them," said Bozo who had been eating the figs and oranges from the containers on the ship.

Oscar glowed again, tapping his beak against the side of the container.

"Hang on," said Bozo as he felt his hand along one of its sides, picking up splinters from the rough wood. He kept silent through the pain for fear of getting caught.

He felt the tiniest bulge at the side where a few of the nails had come loose. Bozo and Andre pulled back the side of the container and crawled into the box. Oscar flew in behind them.

Bozo was sure that Oscar had found the only empty container on the ship. The boys shuffled around in the dark to get comfortable.

“Bozo, I hate small places,” whispered Andre, his breath becomingly increasingly deeper and louder.

“Bozo,” he raised his voice, “I hate this small box.” By this point, Andre was gasping for air.

Bozo grabbed his hands. “I’m beside you, Andre. Relax. Keep breathing, okay?”

“Bozo, I’m scared,” said Andre, almost shouting and breathing so fast Bozo thought he would lose consciousness.

Still holding on to Andre’s hand, Bozo reached over and pushed out the gap through which they had entered to let in a small amount of light.

“Is that any better, Andre?”

“No, Bozo, I’m scared,” said Andre, almost crushing Bozo’s hands with fear. Bozo was terrified that Andre would either scream at the top of his lungs or pass out with fear.

“Oscar!” yelled Bozo in frustration, giving Oscar and Andre a fright. “Oscar, help me out here,” he demanded.

Oscar lifted the lid of the box with his wings and gently slid the lid on top of the other boxes so that they could see the ceiling of the hold and let in some light. Then Oscar landed on Andre’s right shoulder and glowed his golden hue, enough to illuminate the little box, but low enough that the light wouldn’t let the sailors know they had company.

"Is that better, Andre?" asked Bozo.

Andre nodded his head, releasing the force of his grasp. His breathing slowed a little. He didn't have the energy to do any more, as he lay down his head to get some rest with Oscar by his side.

For the next two days, the boys and Oscar were confined to this wooden box. Oscar continued to be their light bulb. They ate only the figs, oranges and water from the nearby boxes. It was difficult to describe how Bozo felt, probably because he still did not feel anything.

"Bozo, are you awake?" asked Andre in a whisper, breaking their long silence.

"No," said Bozo sarcastically.

"Can you let me know when you're awake?"

said Andre sincerely. He didn't get the joke.

"I'm awake now," said Bozo a few moments later, turning to listen to his friend.

"Are we going to die, Bozo?" he asked.

There was silence. Bozo didn't know the answer.

"If I die will you look after Oscar?" Andre continued.

Bozo thought for a few minutes.

"Andre, I don't know what's going to happen to us. But we're friends. We're a team. Me, you and Oscar. We're fighters and we will keep fighting, okay?"

"Thanks, Bozo," said Andre. "I don't want to die. Not today."

Céad Míle Fáilte

A few hours later, Andre woke to the deafening sound of a foghorn and the noise of the cargo boxes being unloaded from the boat.

"Quick, quick," said Andre in a whisper.

Bozo and Andre had to make a fast getaway. The two boys had no idea where they should be going and they both looked to Oscar for direction, but he was too busy eating seeds off the floor.

"Looks like we're on our own with this one," they said to each other. The door of the ship opened and then the big wooden cargo boxes were being lifted out by forklift trucks.

Bozo, Andre and Oscar managed to weave through the cargo boxes and onto shore without anyone seeing them.

They followed the exit signs out of the port, running from large container to large container, knowing that if they were caught they would be sent home and to war. The exit gates of the yard were in sight, and all they had to do was run through those gates without anyone seeing them. They had no idea where they were, what country they were in or even how or when they were to return. The only thing they were interested in today was staying alive.

They were just at the gates to freedom when they heard a voice yelling at them. “Hey! Where are you going to?”

Bozo’s heart sank, certain they’d been caught.

"Those boxes won't move themselves! Now get back to work."

"Phew! Bozo, they think we work here," said Andre. To avoid suspicion, they returned to the boxes and pushed them onto the lorries. When no one was looking, they made a dash for the exit. Oscar wasn't offering any help, and Bozo and Andre just had to figure how to get out of there for themselves. They had just about turned the corner when a security man stepped out in front of them.

"Where are you two off to?" said the six-foot-four, robust man, as he towered over them with his arms folded.

"We're just ... um, we're just ... going home," said Bozo.

"Really?" said the man, who could tell from

their olive skin and foreign accents that they were not locals.

"Where's home?" he asked with one eyebrow raised.

"Um ... well, um ... it's where our house is," said Andre, trying to help Bozo along.

"Your house? Where's your house?" the man asked, not believing a word.

"It's um ... well, it's ... between a lake and the ski resort," said Bozo, describing a picture of a wooden cabin he had seen in a holiday brochure on one of the yachts he worked on.

"Yeah," said Andre, "with loads of palm trees and monkeys." Palm trees and monkeys were always part of Andre's idea of where he'd like to live.

"Palm trees and monkeys? That's a new one.

I've never heard of palm trees and monkeys in Ireland," the man said.

They both looked at each other, a bit embarrassed about their weak lies and about never having heard of a place called Ireland.

"This place is a lot colder than where you are from and we certainly don't have palm trees or monkeys," the guard said, frowning.

"You can't send us home, sir," Andre pleaded.

"I'm afraid that's not a choice I can make. The law is law, and we have to send you home," he said as he grabbed them both by the collar of their shirts and pulled them towards the ship. He knew that they had just come off the boat, which only stopped in Vladislav, so they would have to be sent back there. "Do you see that boat over there?" he said as he pointed to another large cargo ship. “That ship is going to back Vladislav in a few minutes and I’m sending you back to where you came from.”

“You can’t! We’ll be killed,” said Bozo. “Look I can show you” Bozo took out his video recorder to show to the security man but he just ignored it.

“Nonsense, stop exaggerating. Children are always exaggerating.” He dismissed them as though they were being paranoid.

“We’re not exaggerating. We will be killed! You don’t understand,” pleaded Bozo.

“You’ve been reading too many books,” he said as he continued to march over to the boat to inform the captain.

“There’s a boat going back to Vladislav in a few minutes and you two will be on it.”

Andre became hysterical. He screamed so hard that he fell to the floor and screamed like a baby. “You can’t, you can’t, you can’t, you can’t, you can’t,” he yelled, drawing unwelcome attention.

“Okay, okay, stop making a scene, young man. Boys, you can’t stay here. It’s illegal, and if the police find you, you’ll be sent home. If anyone knows that I know you’re here, I’ll lose my job,” said the guard, who was not going to be swayed by a childish tantrum.

Bozo was scrambling to find his video recorder in his jacket pocket to show the security man proof, but before he had time, he was lifted up again and carried over to the cargo ship. The guard said nothing as he dropped them onto the bow of the boat, turned around and walked back to his security cabin beside the exit gate.

Bozo and Andre both looked at Oscar, but he had resumed eating the seeds off the floor.

"Oscar, help us out here. They can't send us home! Do something," said Bozo, but Oscar was oblivious.

"Jump off," yelled the security man racing to the ship. "Jump off!"

The door was closing upwards from the ground and there was just about enough space for the boys to jump through the side. There was about a metre of ocean between the boat and the dock and the metal propellers under the boat were making the water swirl.

Oscar glowed his golden hue and flew out.

Andre jumped over the water and safely onto land.

Looking down at the swirling sea, Bozo imagined falling into the water and being cut to pieces by the steel propeller.

One, two, three, he thought, before jumping safely onto dry land.

"I've just heard on the radio that war has broken out in Vladislav and boys as young as five are being sent to fight. You can't go back there," the security guard said.

"Follow me," he continued. "There's a narrow lane behind those cargo boxes. Keep following that lane for about twenty minutes. It will bring you to a big bridge. Wait on the bridge until you see me. You'll follow me into a warehouse building, but leave a few metres between us. If anyone knows that I know you, I will lose my job. Okay?"

"Okay," the boys agreed.

Andre and Bozo walked in the cold and rain and grey, windy misery of the Irish autumn for what felt like an eternity before they reached the bridge.

They sat waiting, watching the seagulls fly by and the cars pass alongside the river. The two boys were shivering with the cold, their teeth starting to chatter, their feet and hands becoming numb. The security man sure was taking his time to find them.

Finally, they heard a whistle from across the busy road. The guard turned his back on the boys and continued walking up the road, while the boys followed a few yards behind. No one would have suspected that the three were walking as a group.

The man turned left, walked through a large scrap yard full of old machinery, planks of wood, old steel buckets, empty cans, rusty bikes, tennis balls and even a unicycle. He went into an old, grey, stone warehouse that looked like it had been desolate for years. He climbed up some steel stairs, still not waiting for or acknowledging the boys, he then opened the heavy steel door. Inside was a large, cold room. The floor and the walls were stone, and there were two old beds on either side of a mid-sized window and a sweeping brush. There was a sink with some cupboards. Inside the cupboards there were some saucepans and some plates and cutlery, a long mirror, some bedclothes and pillows. There was a light, which Bozo was relieved to see – at least Andre wouldn't be afraid of the dark. And there was a small bathroom.

“I brought you some blankets and clothes and some food. You’ll be safe here. It’s not exactly a palace, but it’ll be a roof over your heads for the next while.”

There was a long, uncomfortable silence. No one knew what to say.

“My name is Gerry” said the man.

“So you’ve come all the way over here to fight for your lives?” Gerry asked.

The boys nodded.

His voice softened. “Well, I have a little boy at home. He’s about your age and he’s fighting for his life, too.”

“I’m sorry to hear that,” said Bozo.

“He’s very sick and he won’t get any better.

He's at home all day in the bed. He can't go out to play like the other kids and he's always in poor form. The medicine is very expensive, so I work all day to keep the money coming in. I barely get to see him anymore. If anyone finds out that I know you're here, I'll lose my job. And if I lose my job, my son won't get his medicine. So promise me that you won't tell anyone you know me," he said.

"We promise," they said together, with Oscar tweeting as though he had understood every word.

"Bozo is a prince," said Andre sincerely.

"*Andre,*" said Bozo, embarrassed. He knew people expected a prince to be royal and rich.

"Really? Pleased to meet you," the man laughed. "Well, Your Majesty, this will be your castle. I'm sorry that you can't come home with me, but I'll go to prison if the gardaí know you're here."

"The who? The gar-dee?" asked Bozo.

"The gardaí. That's the name for the police in Ireland. They wear navy jackets and trousers and blue hats with badges in the middle. If you see them, run. Just stay out of their way, okay?"

"Of course," said Bozo, who was grateful for the warning.

"Now, do you know where you are?" he asked. "This place is called Dublin. And the country is called Ireland," he explained.

"Is this heaven?" asked Andre.

"No son. It's not heaven. But the people are nice, so long as you keep out of trouble and don't do anything bold. If you walk along that river there," he said, pointing out the window, "- that's the River Liffey - and if you walk along it, you'll get to the city where there's loads of shops and music. This place is a lot colder than Vladislav, so make sure you wrap up warm. I brought you some food and some old clothes. They're not exactly 'cool', as the kids say around here. But they'll keep you warm so that you don't get the flu. Can either of you read?"

"I can read," said Bozo.

"Okay, well, I'll leave a note for you when I have any news about the war and when you can go home. Please God, it won't be too long."

"I'm sorry that I can't help you more than that, boys," he said, looking genuinely heartbroken by how little he could offer them.

“I’m Bozo. And this Andre,” said Bozo, “and that is Oscar,” he continued when the bird tweeted hello.

“God bless ye both,” he put his hands on their heads as he walked away. Turning around at the door he said, “Céad míle fáilte, boys.”

“Ceee-ad mee-la fall-tch. What does that mean, Bozo?” Andre asked.

“Never heard it before,” said Bozo.

“It’s an Irish expression and it means ‘a hundred thousand welcomes’.”

The Showman Cometh

That night, after getting some cold soup, fresh bread and a few chocolate biscuits into their bellies, the two boys and Oscar fell asleep. The next morning, when daylight returned, they saw the seagulls as they flew up and down the River Liffey. For a few brief moments, Bozo thought he was back in Port Alexandrov on one of the yachts and it had all been a bad dream. Opening his eyes to reveal the dreary stone wall, he searched the room again only to be disappointed. When he turned around and rubbed the sleep from his eyes, Andre was sitting upright on the side of his bed waiting for

Bozo to wake up.

"We want to go home now, Bozo," said Andre with Oscar sitting still on his shoulder.

Bozo ignored him. What could he say? Unfortunately this situation was no more familiar to Bozo than it was to Andre. At home, Bozo could take charge and know the right thing to do. They were both homesick. Both had lost their families. It wasn't any easier for Bozo than it was for Andre, but Bozo felt he had to be stronger for both their sakes.

"Bozo, we want to go home now," repeated Andre on behalf of himself and Oscar. "We don't like this anymore. We don't like being circus stars anymore. Get up and get dressed and we can go home and be back in time for school tomorrow." Andre walked towards the door and down the stairs of the empty warehouse.

Bozo didn't know how to explain to Andre that they might never go home again and that their families may be dead.

He's serious, thought Bozo, as he ran out the door in a panic to stop him. Apart from not knowing what was safe and what wasn't, Bozo was terrified that if they were caught by the police, or rather the *gardaí*, that they would be sent home and straight to war.

"Andre we have to stay here, just for another little while," he reasoned.

"No," said Andre firmly. "We don't like being famous anymore. We're going home."

"Andre, you can't leave," Bozo shouted after him, following him out to the scrap yard and standing in front of him, blocking his way.

“I can and you can’t stop me,” said Andre as he marched stubbornly past Bozo.

“Andre, *please*,” shouted Bozo. “We have to wait here just a few more days. There are no ships to Valdislav for another few days. Let’s wait here until then.”

Bozo had no idea if they would be there for a few days. For all he knew, they could starve to death in that yard and no one would even miss them. He couldn’t tell Andre that of course, so he would have to think of something fast as Andre and Oscar marched out the door and through the massive scrap yard.

“Oi, what are you two troublemakers doing here?” shouted a burly man from across the busy road.

"Get out of there! You're trespassing and I'll call the gardaí!" he shouted. It was enough to scare Bozo and Andre as they ran around the corner and waited for the man to leave, before they ran back into the yard and up the stairs, where they locked themselves in the warehouse.

"Andre, it's really important that no one knows we're here. We can't talk to strangers, okay? We will go home soon, I promise," said Bozo, trying to reason with him.

"Am I in trouble?" asked Andre, innocently worried that he had been bold.

"No, you're not. But we have to work as a team, okay?" said Bozo.

Andre nodded.

"You too, Oscar," he added.

Oscar tweeted and flapped his wings.

There was a long pause. At first they were quiet because of the scare they'd had, but then boredom took over. The stillness and emptiness of the miserable place gave Bozo and Andre little to talk about. When they looked out the window, there was no colour, no happiness in this grey place. It was a stark contrast to the sunny shores of Vladislav where Bozo, Andre and Oscar longed to be, even if the Mafia were there, too.

"I'm starving," said Andre, holding his stomach.

"Don't worry, we'll get something to eat," said Bozo. Of course, he had no money and no idea where to find food.

"Any ideas, Oscar?" he asked playfully

Oscar chirped and chirped and chirped, so

loudly that Bozo interrupted him.

"Okay, okay, we get the picture. You're hungry too. At least you can fly away and find your food." Bozo opened the window to let Oscar fly over the river.

"Bozo, I'm scared," said Andre.

The enormity of what had happened was overwhelming. Bozo was scared, too. But Bozo had to be the voice of reason and hope.

"Look, Andre, if we can impress Mr. Edwards so much that he wants to make us stars; and if we can escape from those soldiers with guns without getting killed, and get to a country hundreds of miles away, then we can live here until the war is over and we can go home to be with our families."

"Do you think our families are dead?" asked

Andre.

"No," said Bozo.

"Really? They're really alive?" said Andre, excited.

At that moment, for some reason, Bozo firmly believed that their families were still alive.

"Yes, Andre. Your mother is still alive and so are my mother, father, grandmother and Mr. Edwards. And we're going to go back there and find them. You, me and Oscar. I promise."

For once, Bozo really believed what he was saying. "We've done all that, Andre. You, me and Oscar, we've done it as a team and we couldn't have done it on our own. We can do this. Seriously, we can do this." For the first time in days, or maybe in his life, Bozo had fire in his belly and was beginning to think he could win the fight the biggest fight of his life - the fight for himself, Andre, Oscar and his family. He continued, “We’re not quitters. We’re a team. We’ll show them. We’ll be the only two boys from Vladislav to survive the war, and we’ll be heroes, Andre, you and me.”

“And Oscar,” Andre said quickly. “Don’t forget about Oscar.”

“Oscar, of course,” Bozo said sincerely. How could he forget Oscar? He was the third member of the team. Bozo was the leader, Andre was the soldier and Oscar was, well, Oscar was their compass guiding them in the right direction.

By this point, Andre had forgotten about his fear and Bozo was beginning to bounce back to his usual fun-loving self.

Bozo wrapped his bed sheet around his shoulders like a cloak, placed a saucepan upside down on his head, and lifted the broom like a sword. He climbed onto the bed and opened the window, mimicking a king addressing his people from the palace balcony.

“People of Dublin, your prince has arrived,” he said in his mock-posh royal accent.

Andre laughed.

“We have come to rid this country of bad weather, bad manners and uncomfortable beds.”

Andre’s laughing grew louder, which encouraged Bozo to continue with his pantomime.

“I have bought with me two of the finest warriors in all of Vladislav. Andre the Great and

Oscar the ..." Bozo couldn't think of something funny to say, but Andre was delighted to have been mentioned and he rolled on the bed laughing.

"... Oscar the ... the ..." Oscar was chirping like mad as he flew excitedly back to the window.

"Oscar the Golden Winged Warrior! Andre is busy practicing his sword fighting as I speak. His skills know no bounds. Be afraid, all those who dare rise up against the prince. All hail the prince, all hail the prince," Bozo said, banging his broom on the floor as Andre joined in.

Bozo and Andre were enjoying the pantomime so much that, for a few moments, Bozo's black and white world of misery turned into colour.

He lost himself in his imagination, addressing his subjects.

“Bleedin’ shut up, will ya?” roared a voice from outside. It wasn’t an adult voice. Through the window, Bozo spotted three boys the same age as them, on the bank of river.

His heart skipped a beat - firstly, because the unexpected sound gave him a fright, but mainly because it brought him back to reality. He was suddenly acutely aware that he was standing on a windowsill, talking to himself with a saucepan on his head.

“Look at your man with the saucepan on his head,” said a different boy as he pointed and laughed. “He looks ridiculous. Haaa!”

Bozo certainly did look ridiculous and, yes, it was definitely funny, but the boys laughed as loudly as they could just to humiliate him. And they succeeded. Bozo shut the window in a strop.

"Who was that?" said Andre, who could have enjoyed some more.

"Oh, nobody. It's getting cold," said Bozo, not wanting to relive the embarrassment. "Okay, so, food. Let's get some food." He got back down to business, wanting to forget about what had just happened. "Oscar, any ideas?"

Oscar did not glow. In fact, he was a bit temperamental. Great. He had gotten them onto the ship, but Gerry was the one who had organised the room in Dublin. Now they were hungry, with no idea of where they could get food. Bozo was beginning to think Oscar should pull his weight a little bit more. It felt a bit like he was he the only one doing any work around there.

Opportunity Makes the Thief

That evening Bozo decided to venture out to get some food for his new family. He walked out of the warehouse and followed the grey River Liffey straight towards the city of Dublin. He was wearing a blue sweater with a hood, which had on it the crest of a football team he had never heard of. It was dirty and creased and the arms were way too short for him. Nonetheless he was grateful for it in the cold weather.

He walked along the river, trying his best to pull the sleeves down to his wrists and folding his arms tightly to keep himself warm. He searched for some clues as to how he could get some food.

He watched the seagulls swiftly and carelessly flying up and down the river, singing happily. He looked for one of them to turn golden. Why not? Besides, Oscar wasn't coming up with any better suggestions. "It's happened before," he said to himself. And with all the bizarre things that had happened in the last few days, it wouldn't surprise him if he could fly himself. On second thought, maybe not today. He didn't want the humiliation of flapping his arms in full view of everyone, in case it didn't work. With that thought, three swallows swooped over his head and onto the bin just a few metres in front of him. The swallows flew beak first into the bin and, within seconds, had rummaged through and pulled out large pieces of white bread with some ripped slices of meat.

Bozo looked to heaven. “I know that’s one option, God, but ...”

His stomach was beginning to turn at the thought of eating from the bin. “Are you really going to make us eat this?” he continued chatting to himself as he approached the black bin, almost too weak to consider any other option. Just as he approached, the faint daylight caught a glistening object beside the half-eaten sandwiches strewn in the rubbish. Bending down to investigate more, he saw three coins.

Money. Looking to the sky again, he laughed. “That was funny, God. You must be having a good laugh at me up there,” he said, happy to play along with the joke and fully believing that

God had sent the coins to him to buy food. Bozo had no idea how much money he had, but he was sure it was enough to provide them with as much food as they wanted. After all, the accommodation wasn't up to scratch and he was sure he would be compensated with good food. Straight after that thought, another swallow swooped over Bozo's head. Bozo took this as a sign to follow the bird. Sure enough, they took a sharp right turn and there in front of him was a food shop.

Easy, he thought, *plenty of help here*: *Gerry, finding us a place to stay; Oscar - when he isn't too lazy - and now these swallows. Everything's going to be fine*. Bozo felt assured that they were being magically looked after.

"Don't know why we ever worried," he said to

himself, suddenly cheerful.

Bozo picked up a basket for the shopping he was going to bring back to Andre and Oscar. He couldn't wait to tell Andre how he had found the money.

"Definitely treating us today, God," he said as he walked into the small corner shop. Bozo happily walked past the fresh fruit, groceries and salads and straight over to the chocolate cake. He threw five packets of biscuits and a month's supply of bird food for Oscar into the basket, along with bread and cakes and fizzy drinks. He felt sick at the sight of figs and oranges as they reminded him of being on the ship.

Bozo barely succeeded in lifting his overflowing basket onto the tall counter.

A little old lady hobbled her way through a door behind the counter and over to the cash register. She adjusted her glasses and keyed each item into the out-dated machine at a painfully slow speed.

"Hurry on," Bozo wanted to say to her, as he salivated over the biscuits.

"That'll be nineteen pounds, seventy-eight pence, love," she said as she held out her wrinkled hand and forced a smile that revealed her crooked, filthy teeth.

Bozo handed her the three coins as he packed the groceries into the bag.

"Another nineteen pounds, seventy-five pence, love." There was a long silence as her hand stayed outstretched.

"What?" said Bozo, confused.

"The rest of it. Sure that's only three pence. You won't get much for three pence around here, love. Maybe a few jellies," she said as she pointed to the box of jellies on the counter

"But that's all I have," said Bozo, pulling out his empty pockets to prove it.

"Go way out a that, love, will ya?" she started to laugh. It was embarrassing that he didn't have more money but, worse, he was starving.

"You're having a laugh with me, ya cheeky bugger. Get out of the shop before I call the gardaí and have ya arrested," she said.

Is everyone here afraid of the gardaí? he thought. They mentioned them a lot.

The old lady started muttering to herself as she grabbed the sweeping brush to shoo him out of the shop. "I'm sick of ye smart alecks coming in here," she said as she chased him. "Get out, will ya." She started to poke him with the brush. "Get out, ya little thug. The cheek of ya, coming in here with only three pence."

Bozo was scared, but he still hadn't forgotten about his belly. He grabbed one of the bags of food off the counter. He kicked the old lady in the shin and ran out of the shop as fast as his legs would carry him, heading down the Liffey where hundreds of cars were now parked along both sides of the road. He ran through the hundreds of people who were walking in the direction of his new home. He didn't look back, even when he heard the shouts of people running after him. *The gardaí. They're crawling around here*. He didn't stop or look back until he had safely reached the front door of the warehouse. He didn't even wait to climb the stairs, either. He sat on the first step and bit into the yummiest, crumbliest chocolate chip cookie.

Having finished the packet and feeling a slight pang in his belly from eating too fast and a slight pang in his consciousness for stealing food, Bozo burst through the door with an uncontainable excitement.

"Andre, Oscar, guess what happened?" he called. There was no answer. "Hello?" He paused. "Where are you?" he asked as he searched under the two beds. "Oh no." He panicked. "Have they gone home?"

Just as he was leaving to search for them, he heard a commotion outside his window. Bozo opened the window to see that thousands and thousands of people were walking into the building next door. They were carrying flags, banners, whistles and hats. He walked out, against the flow of the crowds coming towards him.

'Excuse me' he asked a stranger, but where is everyone going to?'

'There's a Laois versus Dublin football match on," said the stranger, putting a woollen hat on Bozo's head. "We need all the support we can get. If anyone asks you who you're supporting say, 'C'mon, Laois!'"

"Come on, Laois," Bozo responded with a laugh and continued to walk against the traffic along the side of the road, looking for Andre and Oscar. Then he saw the three boys who had laughed at him yesterday, pointing and directing drivers into parking spaces along the road. What interested Bozo the most was that they looked like they were getting money for each car they helped to park.

Bozo knew this was an easy job and it would be a great way for him and Andre to make money. He heard Andre's voice in the distance. He looked up along the long road by the river to see Andre and a golden-glowing Oscar collecting their pound notes for doing the same simple job.

"Oh, *now* you go golden," said Bozo to himself, annoyed that Oscar could have thought of that idea before he nearly got arrested for stealing.

More Trouble

Andre and Oscar had received their fortieth pound note, having parked their fortieth car. Well, actually it was thirty-nine-and-a-half pound notes. One shrewd businessman had handed them a pound and then taken it back, before tearing it in half and promising to give back the second half when he returned and his car was safely where he had left it.

Down the road, the three Irish boys were busy providing the same service, when they must have realised that their takings were a little short that day.

“What’s the diagnosis, Brains?” asked Elvis, the self-appointed King of the Inner City. His character was similar to his idol Elvis. The name Elvis was a little more rock 'n' roll than his real name, which was Ian. However, the two characters had a few things in common. For a start, they were both very good-looking and they knew it. They both also spoke with an American accent. Ian, however, had learnt his off the TV. They both had jet-black hair combed back tightly at the sides and with a large quiff in the centre. They both wore long, tight dark-blue jeans, tight white T-shirts and a black leather jackets with the collar turned up. Ian had dark brown eyes and milky clear skin. His face was very handsome and he knew it.

"I bet you there is somebody else doing the same as us," Brains responded, quickly working it out that by this time they usually would have earned one hundred and thirty pounds.

“What? You mean there’s someone better looking than me here?” asked Elvis, totally shocked by the news.

“No, Elvis. There’s someone parking cars and taking our money.”

“What? We’ve been robbed,” said Elvis as he checked his pockets. “The money’s here, stupid,” he said as he pulled out his ninety pounds. “We haven’t been robbed,” he laughed, mocking his friend. “I don’t know why they call you Brains ...”

“No, Elvis, there’s someone else parking cars and taking the money that should be ours,” said Sniffer, the third member of the gang. Brains had so christened him because of his razor sharp ability to source information, like the sniffer dogs who worked on the docks sniffing out illegal drugs or guns or anything that shouldn't be imported into the country.

"Oh, I know what you mean," Elvis said, although he was a little embarrassed. "What are you standing there for, Sniffer? Go and find out who's taking our money." His embarrassment changed to anger and a need to reassert himself as the leader of the gang. "And fast!" he yelled.

"Yes, boss," said Sniffer, as he scurried off to find the culprit. He didn't have to scurry too far to find Andre, Bozo and Oscar.

Elvis, Sniffer and Brains approached Bozo and Andre, who were minding their own business, concentrating on not being caught by the gardaí, and making sure the drivers didn't bang into anybody else's car.

"Hey fellas. Let me introduce myself. I am Ian, but my friends call me Elvis because of my good looks," he said, straightening up the collar on his leather jacket. He really did love himself.

"And these boys here are my sidelicks," said Elvis, charmingly.

"Sidekicks," whispered Brains to Elvis trying to be discrete, although everyone heard him.

"Yeah, that's what I said, sidekicks. I think you need to get your hearing checked out," said Elvis dropping his charming façade in a temper.

"This is Sniffer and this is Brains." He pointed at them for introduction. He had gotten the names the wrong way around, but they didn't want to correct their ringleader again.

"And you, my friend, are on our turf. We're

giving you five seconds to leave. Ready?" said Elvis as he clicked his fingers in the air. Brains knew to count on cue.

"One, two, three ..." Brains counted.

Bozo knew that the money had been far too easy to come by and couldn't last. He always wimped out around bullies, and at this point he would have been quite happy to keep doing it and run home with the forty pounds in their pockets before the boys counted to five.

"Yeah? Says who?" Andre had never stood up for himself before now and Oscar had started beaming golden which always meant it was time to get out of there.

"Says me," said Elvis, as he squared up to Andre, pushing his nose on his face.

"Five," shouted Brains, followed by Elvis

punching Andre, whose head hit the ground. His glasses fell off and broke. Andre fought back, punching and punching, but it was like throwing toothpicks at a grizzly bear. He was being blasted by a tsunami of punches from Elvis. Bozo tried a few of his karate-style kicks into Elvis's back as Oscar continued to glow.

"I'll grab that guy's arm, you grab the other one," shouted Brains to Sniffer, quickly realising that if they both held onto Bozo's arms then Elvis could fight Andre some more.

Bozo lifted up his arms and punched them both in the face with his clenched fists. He managed to hit them both, but they didn't release him from their grasp.

A crowd had swelled and some adults stepped in to break up the fight.

"What's going on here, fellas?" asked a man in a blue jacket and hat with a badge in the middle.

"Nothing, garda," said Elvis. "We were just messing around with our new friends here."

"Really?" he said, his forehead creasing in disbelief.

"Have these boys being causing you trouble?" the garda asked Bozo and Andre.

It was their perfect time to say yes, these boys had come over to beat them up, which surely was against the law in every country in the world. Now was the perfect time to tell the garda everything and for once justice would be served and the bullies would be put in prison, or at least punished.

But of course they needed to keep their mouths

shut if they didn't want to be sent home.

"I've warned you before, Ian. If I catch you in trouble again, I'll send you to prison. Do you hear me?"

"Yes, Garda Teapot," Elvis muttered the word "Teapot" under his breath. He'd earned his nickname because of his long nose and big sticky-out ears. Brains and Sniffer sniggered quietly at the bravery of their leader.

"What did you say?" The officer bent down and pushed his teapot nose into Elvis's face.

I said, "Yes, Garda."

"You'd better, because I'm warning you now. If I catch you in trouble again ..." He looked around, terrifying Bozo and Andre. "If I catch any of you in trouble again, I'll be sending you all to jail. Now off with you all."

With those words the boys scarpered.

Where Do We Go to from Here?

The money from helping cars to park at the football match saw the boys through a few weeks. They had become accustomed to eating warm, greasy bags of chips and battered cod, fresh from the Irish Sea, with loads of tomato ketchup and loads and loads of salt and vinegar. It was the only thing about Ireland they liked. The next few weeks were difficult for the boys. They didn't know where to turn to next and they were running out of money. Every day they looked out the window, hoping that another football match would happen, and sometimes it did. But they could only make a small amount of money before they were chased by not just Elvis, Sniffer and Brains, but also their cousins and friends who didn't want the competition. It wasn't just Vladislav that was full of bullies. Bozo realised they must be everywhere. He knew he couldn't spend the rest of his life running scared from these boys. However, how he was going to tackle that issue was another story.

Bozo and Andre were both homesick, but they made a pact not to speak about it.

Of course, they still had to buy the essentials, even though they tried desperately to live within their meagre means. But those short sleeves and worn shoes let the rain in and the weather was becoming very wintry, so they bought themselves some new clothes to keep themselves warm and dry. They also bought themselves five blankets each for their beds. They were sure that some days it was warmer outside than it was inside. The empty stone building never seemed to heat up. In comparison to the blazing heat in Vladislav, Ireland was unbelievably cold and being on their own made it seem all the more miserable. However, every morning they had a routine. Their bodies from the neck down were warm and toasty, as they were wrapped in five wool blankets. But their noses were always pink with the cold and they could see their breath.

“Are you awake, Bozo?” Andre would ask every morning.

“Yeah, just two more minutes,” Bozo would reply. He knew what was coming and wanted to enjoy his bed for a bit longer.

"Come on, Bozo, we'll have to do it sooner or later," Andre would say. "Come on, one, two, three!"

They would both pull back their blankets, jump out of bed and straight into jumping jacks. They jumped up and down, their legs moving left and right, their hands clapping above their heads.

They hated the first few seconds. It always reminded Bozo of when he would first get into the sea. There was no way to avoid the cold. You just had to hold your breath and dip your head into the water.

Twenty jumping jacks later, they would sprint on the spot while Andre counted to twenty. He always did it as fast as he could speak and missed a few numbers along the way, accidentally on purpose.

After that, they did twenty jumps into the air while lifting their knees to their chest. By this point their bodies were beginning to warm up.

The next daily routine was to look for a note left by Gerry to say that the war was over, but it was never there and their hearts sank every time.

"Any notes today?" Andre would ask.

"Not today, Andre. Maybe tomorrow," was always Bozo's reply, but he was beginning to wonder if Gerry had forgotten about them.

The night before Bozo's birthday, he cried himself to sleep. When he was in Slavlov he used to imagine that his tenth birthday would be celebrated on a yacht as a circus superstar and as far away from Slavlov and the Mafia as he could get. Now there was nowhere he would rather be. He knew that tomorrow there would be no cake, no bicycles, no show, no presents, no annoying neighbours, no friends - not even the Mafia. Nothing. Bozo feared he would never return home and never see his family again.

That morning Andre and Oscar were waiting for Bozo to wake.

“Bozo,” called Andre very softly, ever so gently trying to wake him. Andre had been sitting for hours at the side of the bed.

“Bozo,” he called gently as Bozo opened his eyes from his deep sleep. Oscar helped him with a gentlest chirp.

“Happy birthday, Bozo. You’re my best friend,” said Andre as he held out his hand, poked up his glasses that he had taped together after the fight with Elvis, and handed Bozo a kite from behind his back.

Bozo had no idea where Andre got the money to buy a kite or even how he remembered his birthday, but it lifted Bozo's spirits so much that again he just knew they were not on their own and they were definitely going to get home.

Roll Up, Roll Up!

That morning, Bozo jumped out of bed with a renewed sense of enthusiasm. He made his bed, took his last five pounds out of the tin can they used as a bank and ran down to the shops to buy Andre, Oscar and himself a hearty breakfast.

After breakfast Bozo balanced on a short plank of wood that was perched on a rolling pipe, while juggling seven empty bean cans and singing one of his cheerful performance songs. Andre and Oscar chirped and sang along. After finishing his song, Bozo caught the first can with the tip of his toe, the second with the tip of another toe, then four in the hat that was on his head. The last he caught on his forehead, then flipped it onto the tip of his nose. As it was about to fall off, he flipped it again high into the air. Oscar chirped and chirped around it, playing with it. It landed on Oscar's wing. He flipped it off one wing, onto his other wing, then he flipped it again and it landed in Bozo's hat.

"Bravo, bravo," shouted Andre, thoroughly enjoying being the audience. He loved it when Bozo entertained them. It always ended with Andre laughing so hard that Bozo would have to stop to allow him to catch his breath. Bozo loved the way Andre could just stop and enjoy things. Here they were in this hellhole and Andre and Oscar seemed, just for a few moments, to forget about how miserable their lives were.

“Okay, m’lord,” he said to Andre, still in character, “the servants have been cooking all morning and they have baked some delicious fluffy crusty bread all the way from Pluto. And some ham all the way from the moon, and cheese all the way from the farthest galaxy in the stars. Please be seated.”

Bozo had made a table out of some old wooden boxes and turned some bottle crates upside down to use as stools. He fluffed up a pillow for effect. He was wearing the saucepan on his head as a crown.

“You are the prince’s best friend and today we shall eat like kings.”

After they had filled their bellies until they

could eat no more, they spent the morning running up and down the Liffey, playing with Bozo's new kite.

"Let's go into the city," said Bozo.

"But won't we get caught? asked Andre, trying to obey the rules that Bozo had set when they had arrived in Ireland.

"Nonsense! Today there are no rules, Andre."

Bozo and Andre and Oscar went across the bridge to a very posh shopping street called Grafton Street.

Today they were not going to be apologetic and poor like they had been since they arrived. They were there to show Dublin that they belonged there.

Dublin was magical. It was crisp and wintry. For the first time, the boys could see the beauty in this weather. The sharpness of the cold and the small flakes of snow made this place special. It was even more beautiful than if it had been sunny. The fairy lights were shaped like chandeliers and there were street entertainers outside most of the shops.

The boys spotted a vacant spot outside a very posh and busy restaurant. They took their place on the street and started performing their circus acts. They left their woollen hats on the floor to collect money.

“We’re going home soon,” said Bozo. “I just know we are. I can feel it.”

Who's That Girl?

Everywhere Bozo, Andre and Oscar found a way they could make some money, Elvis, Sniffer and Brains had the same idea. Street performing on Grafton Street in the winter was one money-making opportunity everyone knew about. Bozo had heard a passer-by refer to it as busking. Bozo, Andre and Oscar had spotted Elvis, Brains and Sniffer but they were a comfortable distance away and they were too busy performing their acts and playing the violin to get into a fight ... yet.

In between where Bozo and Elvis were performing, Bozo noticed a string quartet of female musicians that looked around his age who all arrived on Grafton Street at eleven o'clock. They all wore black and played their instruments beautifully. Two played the violin, one played the viola and another played the cello, reading their music sheets from their music stands. Bozo thought they sounded very good but they looked very serious.

"How'ya, Aoife? You look gorgeous today. Will you be me girlfriend?" shouted Elvis to one of the musicians as they had just completed one of their classical pieces of music.

She is very pretty, thought Bozo. Aoife had long, wavy, dark hair. Her skin was the colour of cream, and she had the lightest, most beautiful, big green eyes and a beautiful face. She looked straight ahead, ignoring the comments she received from Elvis as if he was so beneath her that he didn't exist. It was Halloween and the schools were on mid-term break. Every day over the break, the three groups would perform on Grafton Street, and every day Elvis, Sniffer and Brains would walk by her just to talk to her, sometimes bringing their own instruments to serenade her.

They had a game: if she looked over, they got one point. If she looked over and smiled, it was two points. If she spoke to them then they won bag of chips which the other two had to pay for. But they never scored any points, because Aoife simply ignored them. Except for today.

Bozo watched as Aoife finished busking. Her head was held high, and staring straight in front of her, she walked past them. She stopped, turned around, marched past their box of money, and walked over to Elvis, looking straight into his face. He closed his eyes and pouted his lips for a kiss. She pulled his violin off him, turned the tuning pegs on the top and shoved it back into his hand.

"If I am going to have to listen to you group of losers every day for the rest of the holidays, then at least your instruments will be in tune."

'You've changed, Aoife. You used to be in our gang. Now that your dad's got a bit of money you're too good for us,' said Elvis.

Bozo didn't like Elvis but he could see that Aoife thought she was far too good for him.

'I was never in your gang. And I am not from where you're from any more. I am doing this for charity, not for pocket money," said Aoife before she walked to her chauffeured car. The chauffeur, dressed in a black suit and black hat, opened the door for her.

Bozo, Andre and Oscar watched the whole scene with amusement. They liked Aoife and loved that she put those boys in their place. But just as Aoife was about to get into the car, a very attractive blonde lady stepped into the car from the other side. She looked over her shoulder at the commotion on Grafton Street.

Bozo and Andre looked at each other, stunned.

“It’s Sandy!”

From Black and White into Colour

"My hands are sore," complained Andre as he carried the end of a plank of wood under his arm and two steel buckets containing some tennis balls in his hands.

"We're nearly there, Andre; it's just around the corner," said Bozo as he carried the front piece of the plank of wood in one hand and a unicycle in the other.

The two boys and Oscar turned the corner onto Grafton Street where they placed each end of the plank of wood on the steel buckets, which they had put upside down on the ground.

Bozo was going to do the same circus act he

had practiced with his father deep in the woods. Once the plank of wood was in place, he cycled his unicycle across the plank and juggled his tennis balls at the same time. He could even hop onto a windowsill or a chair while still juggling his tennis balls on his unicycle.

"But what if you fall?" said a nervous Andre.

"I won't fall, Andre. I never have," said Bozo, who was right. He never fell doing that trick.

"But you could fall and have to go to the hospital, and then we will be found out and we'll be sent home to go to war," said Andre.

"It'll be fine. Now we have to wait until Aoife comes. What time is it now?" They looked at the clock above the posh shops of Grafton Street. "Ten minutes to go."

"How are we ever going to talk to Aoife?" asked

Andre.

“We’ll just do the most amazing circus acrobatics and magic tricks of our lives. She’ll notice us and come over to talk to us, we’ll become her friend, meet Sandy and get home,” said Bozo confidently.

“Do you fancy her?” asked Andre innocently.

Oscar looked at Bozo, too.

“No,” said Bozo, blushing, “I hate girls. Okay, now make sure you start singing at eleven,” he said, trying to change the subject.

The street clock chimed eleven times. Aoife, as punctual as ever, walked ever so properly with her friends over to the same spot, where they played their instruments to the delight of many who stopped to listen.

In the meantime Andre played the harmonica

while Oscar chirped along and Bozo juggled on his unicycle, bunny hopping off the plank onto the ground, around the plank and back up onto it again. It was enough to make the crowd cheer and clap along. Everyone was nervous for Bozo's safety, and that made the act even more exciting. Bozo and Andre had definitely attracted the largest crowd of all of the buskers. Bozo loved the feeling of entertaining people. He loved how they cheered as he sprang from the ground onto the plank and up onto the dustbin and back down to the ground again. For the first time in this awful and unbelievable ordeal, he had forgotten about himself and his worries.

Bozo noticed how every so often Aoife would look over to the swelling crowd cheering him on. When her hour of performing was up she walked over to see more of Bozo and this intriguing spectacle. She meandered her way through the swelling crowd and stood right beside Andre as she looked up at Bozo in a trance. For the first time, Bozo noticed that Aoife was smiling, and more importantly she was smiling at him.

Wow she is the prettiest girl I have ever seen in my life, thought Bozo, who was so entranced by her beauty when she smiled at him that he almost lost his balance and fell off the plank. He could feel his face turn red and he became nervous knowing that Aoife was watching.

“What’s his name?” Aoife asked Andre.

“Bozo. He’s a prince,” replied Andre.

“Wow, a prince, a real prince!” said Aoife.

"Bozo doesn't fancy you," said Andre very quickly and then returned to playing his harmonica. "He hates girls." Andre was only repeating what Bozo had said.

"My name is Bozo," the bouncing prince said as he jumped off the unicycle to speak to her. "Pleased to meet you."

Aoife blushed. The crowd cheered. Bozo was delighted.

"Aoife, your car is ready," interrupted a man dressed in a suit. Bozo recognised him as being Aoife's chauffeur.

"Hello, my name is Aoife. I am your new girlfriend." She blew him a kiss and then ran back to her car.

"WOOOOOwwww!" the crowd cheered. Oscar was so excited that he flew around in circles, chirping loudly to Aoife and then to Bozo in turns. He was fully golden.

You've Changed

The following week was mostly a blur for Bozo, who just couldn't wait to see his new girlfriend again on Saturday. He secretly did like Aoife but he didn't want Andre to know this.

"Are you in love?" Andre asked.

"No," Bozo spat back firmly, as though love was a dirty word.

"I mean, yeah, she's my first girlfriend, but she's nothing special. Besides, we're only getting to know her so that we can get to Sandy," Bozo continued, trying to be cool and take it all in his stride.

Andre was confused by his answer. He had

noticed a big difference in Bozo over the past few days. For one, he jumped out of bed every morning. No more lying about for ages. And he acted out funny pantomimes every day, which Andre and Oscar thoroughly enjoyed.

If all that wasn't enough, he mentioned Aoife at every given opportunity, even to strangers when it was totally unrelated to the topic being discussed.

For example, Bozo and Andre had gone to a burger restaurant the day after Aoife had blown him a kiss.

"Hi, can I order a strawberry milkshake, fries and a chicken burger with no lettuce?" Andre had asked, though at this point they were regulars at the place and the waitress had written down their orders before they even spoke. She always brought over a plate of breadcrumbs for Oscar. This was their ritual every time they visited the diner and Andre was beginning to think that the waitress should just bring over their food without them ordering it. However, this was the only place that would let Oscar in, and that was after a long quarrel with the manager, so he kept his mouth shut about the ordering process.

"Can I order the same?" asked Bozo, repeating the request in a robotic trance. "Actually," he considered, breaking with tradition and grabbing the attention of everyone there, including Oscar, who was staring at him intently, "on second thought, *my girlfriend, Aoife,* might prefer me to eat better. So I'll order a salad instead, thanks."

The mention of her name was simply to brag about having a girlfriend. Andre and Oscar looked at the waitress, who looked confused by it all. Andre handed back the menus, his facial expression saying, "Sorry about that." Clearly, Bozo was losing it.

The food arrived and Andre tried to make small talk with his friend, but he was greeted with careless responses, so he just gave up. He decided that Bozo was becoming very moody.

"Why don't you have a girlfriend, Andre? You've never had a girlfriend," said Bozo.

The comment hurt Andre's heart like a train crashing into his chest. He felt belittled. He was left red-faced, almost needing to catch his breath. This wasn't something that he and Bozo had discussed before. Besides, Bozo always said he hated girls, so what was the big deal? But it was Bozo's tone that bothered Andre the most. He said it as though he was all high and mighty, as if he was some sort of macho man just because he now had a girlfriend.

"I don't know," answered Andre, who just wanted to get off the topic, as this whole thing was changing his friend and he didn't like it. Plus, this was becoming a regular occurrence with Bozo. Like the time Andre asked him to perform on Grafton Street with him to make money for some new shoes he badly needed. Normally, Bozo would to help Andre. But instead he had taken to giving lame excuses like, it was a bit cold or he didn't feel the best. But Andre decided to challenge him. He told Bozo that they needed to make money.

"Besides," he continued, "my feet are always wet and ... atchoo!" His sentence went unfinished as he sneezed, but he didn't need to say much more. Andre was beginning to get sick and it meant that it was becoming more of a struggle for him to walk to the shops or do his magic tricks. But Bozo was too self-absorbed to notice.

Game On

Bozo thought the next day would never come, so impatient was he to see Aoife again. Although the weather was becoming colder and darker, Bozo was beginning to see Dublin with fresh eyes. As the days grew darker there were fairy lights in the shape of enormous chandeliers suspended in the middle of Grafton Street. The noise of the bustling crowds doing their shopping added a familial atmosphere, and the musicians dotted along the sides of the famous pedestrian street whipped people into a flurry of merriment and goodwill.

And of course Bozo - Prince Charming himself -

and his assistants, Andre and Oscar, were working their magic. At ten minutes to eleven, Bozo, Oscar and Andre arrived just in time to draw a huge crowd. The plan was to impress Aoife again so that they could meet Sandy and get home.

However, when they arrived, the best position had already been taken by their enemies. The one thing they hadn't considered was Elvis, Sniffer and Brains' determination not to be beaten, either by taking their popularity or taking their girl.

Elvis, Sniffer and Brains had arrived early to nab the best spot on the street. They had spent the whole day before practicing and they had upped their game. Bozo and Andre had spent the whole day before fighting. Today Elvis,

Sniffer and Brains were putting on a break dancing show and the crowds had gathered to watch. Every back flip, spin and dance move to Elvis's impressive beat-boxing skills was applauded by the growing crowd.

Elvis: 1, Bozo: 0

Andre pulled out his harmonica and Bozo commenced his new act, which he had been practicing all night. Using the metal buckets and tin cans from the scrap yard, Bozo had created an act that he knew would be a crowd pleaser. Placing the first bucket upside down, Bozo turned himself upside down and balanced himself on the base of the bucket with his hands. Andre then handed him a slightly smaller bucket which Bozo placed upside down, on top of the first bucket and jumped on top of the base of the second bucket; remaining upside down. He continued to do this, each time the buckets became smaller and smaller until he finished his act balancing his whole body on an empty tin can with one hand and still upside down.

The timing was just right for the crowd to switch their interest to another channel of magic and make believe. Bozo and Andre had stolen the crowd and Oscar was tweeting and flying, enjoying the competition.

Elvis: 1, Bozo: 1.

The clock chimed eleven o'clock and Aoife marched over to the impressively large crowd, head held high, past her annoying admirer and over to her new boyfriend. She was taken aback by size of the audience. Elvis jumped out in front of her with his two sidekicks and the three of them danced to try to get her attention. The crowd cheered their attempts to win the girl.

Everyone was impressed, apart from Aoife, who looked at Elvis with cold eyes. “Excuse me,” she said, as she brushed past them as though she were shooing away an annoying bee.

“Hey, Aoife, why take second prize when you can have first?” Elvis yelled. Unflinching, Aoife froze him out as she walked towards Bozo as though the tough guys weren’t even there.

Elvis: 1, Bozo: 2.

“We can’t lose this, guys, not to that twerp,” Elvis declared.

That twerp was now balancing on five buckets.

“Brains, think of something. What are we going

to do?" said Elvis.

"Hey, girl, you're the prize,

Beautiful, Intelligent; big green eyes.

I am funny, I am fine,

Drop that looser,

And be mine."

Elvis rapped with Brains and Sniffer beat-boxing a rhythm.

Aoife stopped, flicked her hair back and turned to Elvis. She spoke coldly. "I really don't think any of you downtown boys are my type. I prefer princes." She pointed to Prince Bozo himself as he was building his pyramid of steel buckets in the air.

"Ouch," said Elvis playfully, clenching his fists and pretending to stab himself in chest. He then fell to his knees. The crowd cheered. This boy was not giving up. He continued:

“My Heart is broken,
The wounds are deep,
Without your love,
I will forever weep.”

“Awwww,” cheered the crowd. But Aoife ignored him and made her way through the crowds to Bozo.

“A prince? Are ya bleedin’ mad or what? Him, Prince Saucepan Head himself?” shouted Sniffer. “Oh yeah, he’s a prince alright. Wait until you see his castle,” he yelled into the air. Aoife was far too enthralled with Bozo to hear. The crowd laughed, finding humour in this war between the two boys for the affections of this beauty. Sniffer being Sniffer had found out the whole story. He knew that Bozo and Andre were poor refugees, with no parents, here illegally, living from day to day, hand to mouth, stealing from old ladies. They were far from being royal.

“Your type wouldn’t know what a castle was,” Aoife quipped.

“You need to get glasses, love, if you think he’s a prince.” Sniffer may have been able to sniff out information, but his lack of charm let him down. He didn’t realise that talking to Aoife that way did him no favours.

“Well, you need to get a hearing aid if you lot think you can sing. And your type should refer to him as Your Royal Highness,” she said, flicking her hair back.

“She’s gorgeous when she’s cross, isn’t she?” said the ever-so-charming Elvis, who was enjoying the challenge and the smart comments.

“I know we’ve had our first fight, but I’ll make it up to ya, love, I promise,” Elvis said cheekily. At this point, the crowd turned its attention to the developing love triangle between Elvis, Aoife and Bozo who was trying to balance on the final tin.

Oblivious to the hundreds of spectators, Aoife marched up and stood beside Andre, who was playing his harmonica while Oscar chirped in harmony.

“Hello, Prince Bozo,” she called, loud enough to make her presence known, but shyly enough to maintain her charm.

Bozo had been anticipating this moment with such excitement all night that his nerves got the better of him. He had imagined how he would jump to the ground almost like a knight descending from the heavens to meet his princess.

“How-a-ya,” said Bozo in a tough Dublin accent he had never used before. It surprised even him once it had slipped out. He was just so nervous that he started to over think everything. Aoife was a little taken back by the accent. Bozo’s face turned beetroot red and his hands started trembling. He had built up this moment so much that he was terrified to speak.

“How are you ... boyfriend?” Aoife said with knowing smile and a wink.

Andre was hanging on to Bozo and Aoife’s every word so closely that he had forgotten to keep the music playing. Elvis, Sniffer and Brains were too interested to keep their gig going either, and for the next few moments this casual conversation between Aoife and Bozo was watched with anticipation and silence by everyone on the street. Bozo jumped to the ground and was too focused on trying to say something that he didn't notice they were being watched as if it was a television drama.

"Yeah," said Bozo, who was delighted to even be able to even manage that one word without choking with fear.

"Yeah," wasn't exactly answering her question, but at least it was a word. The whole night, Bozo had pictured how he would perform a trick for her; how the crowds would cheer and she would be in awe. Then they would go for a walk and talk about their interests and hobbies. She would be so impressed by this amazing multi-talented person that she would bring him home to her house to show him off, where he would meet Sandy, who would agree to send them home and find his parents. Then he and Andre would be reunited with their families.

"What's it like being a prince?" asked Aoife, who was completely in love with the idea that her boyfriend was an actual, real-life prince. Bozo could hardly speak the truth, but thinking up a lie was just too much for him at that moment. It didn't help that Andre and Oscar looked at him as though he'd had his tongue chopped off. His eyes stared at the ground for what felt like an eternity, while his voice wasn't able to muster a single syllable.

Aoife looked at him, hoping for a few more words.

The long pause was excruciatingly painful as it was shared by the hundreds who had gathered along Grafton Street.

“I don’t think royalty are supposed to say too much in public. It’s not protocol,” the crowd whispered to explain the silence. This travelled around the crowd and over to Aoife.

“Oh yes. Oh, of course,” said Aoife apologetically, curtsying to repair any fault on her part for offending a monarch.

Andre looked on, puzzled. Not familiar with social etiquette himself, he nudged Bozo with his elbow. “Say something to her, Bozo. You’ve been talking about her all night.” His voice carried through the silence of the crowd. Bozo still looked like a rabbit in headlights.

"He really fancies you, Aoife. He tells everybody, even strangers, that you're his new girlfriend, and he has been in a much better mood," said Andre.

"Aaaawwww ..." The crowd sounded like an old lady pinching a toddler's cheek.

Oh no, this is so awkward. I feel like such an idiot, were the only words running through Bozo's mind. He went from feeling like a true prince of the circus to a shy toddler who wanted to hide. Andre's words and the reaction of the crowd exacerbated the awkwardness of the situation until Bozo just wanted the ground to open up and swallow him. His dreams of heroics were now dwarfed by sheer terror, which was clear to everybody, most of all Elvis.

"Hey, Aoife, you need a real man, someone who can talk your language, not some loser that's intim ... intim ..." shouted Elvis, who always had the courage to speak but lacked the intelligence to know what to say.

"What's that word, Brains? Come on, you should be helping me here," he whispered as though it was Brains' fault.

"Intimidated, boss," he responded immediately.

"Yeah, that one. Intim ... intim," Elvis got stuck again.

"Not afraid of you," whispered Brains, who thought of something that was less of a tongue twister.

"Yeah, I'm not afraid of you," said Elvis, but the moment had gone and it just sounded like the wrong thing to say to a girl.

Bozo was intimidated by both of them at this point. For the first time ever, Bozo wished for Elvis's warrior spirit. He was beginning to think that Elvis was the better man, and he wanted to run home, get into bed, cover his head and forget the whole thing. He just felt like he was out of his depth, telling a lie he couldn't live up to, in a battle he couldn't fight.

"Hit it, Sniffer," shouted Elvis, who clicked his fingers. Brains and Sniffer started to play music. Elvis threw off his baseball hat and tore off his baggy hoodie to reveal a smart black long-sleeved T-shirt. He kicked off his trainers and started Irish dancing in his black socks. The crowd formed a circle around Elvis and Aoife as he danced in a circle as though he were performing a ritual dance to win the heart of this girl. He circled her confidently; his legs kicked in the air; his arms on his waist, showing off and fighting for what he wanted.

His seduction began to work. Aoife blushed as she looked into his eyes and she cherished the attention from all who watched. The crowd cheered as Elvis finished and, in a matador-like motion, signalled to Bozo to bring it on. The prize was Aoife's heart.

Elvis: 2, Bozo: 2

Elvis got points for pouncing on an opportunity when his opponent was faltering.

This was providing a huge entertainment for the crowd, who were cheering on the attempts of these determined young suitors.

Bozo stood still, frozen and afraid. He could

feel Andre willing him on, wishing to get home. Oscar flashed golden beside him. He knew the sign never led him astray, but Bozo didn't have the courage to fight.

"You're not going to just stand there and let him take her, are you? Come on, Your Highness, let's see you defend what's yours!" shouted a voice from the crowd.

"Prince Bozo! Prince Bozo! Prince Bozo!" The crowd cheered him on.

"Ready, Oscar?" shouted Andre. Oscar tweeted three times and Andre started playing his music, giving Bozo no time to shy away. Bozo circled Aoife with his elbows in the air and his hands across his chest. "One, two, three, hoy!" the crowd cheered as they clapped along to Andre's harmonica. Bozo flipped into the air and down again. Tap dancing, flipping, clicking his heals in the air, dwarfing the efforts of Elvis.

Elvis: 2, Bozo: 3

“My hero,” said Aoife dreamily. She was delighted that her Prince Charming had stepped up to win her heart.

Bonus points for Bozo. Elvis and his cronies left the playing field beaten, but not defeated.

Aoife joined Bozo and started playing her violin beside Andre and his music box. Bozo continued to do his tricks.

“Sniffer, find the gardaí and tell them that we have some illegal visitors on Grafton Street,” said Brains, thinking of a new strategy quickly.

“Where are you from and what are you doing in Dublin?” Aoife asked Bozo, who was too nervous to stand and talk to her. So he started the act with his buckets again.

"I don't really like talking about it," said Bozo.

"Bozo, you're so private," said Aoife, laughing. "It's okay. My father mixes with royalty all the time. Are your parents here on business? Is it a foreign affairs matter? It's always foreign affairs."

"Foreign affairs?" repeated Bozo. "Well, I guess you could say that."

"Sorry to spoil the party, Aoife," Frederick the chauffeur interrupted. "Your father is finished early today and is waiting in the car for you. We have to go."

"Oh, I have to go now," Aoife told Bozo, "but my father is having a reception in our house tomorrow evening. Would you like to be my date?"

Date! Almost falling off his buckets, Bozo told himself not to blow it again. He was focused on staying upside down and not falling off, but he still had to say something appropriate.

"Yes!" he shouted. It was the only thing he could think of saying without getting tongue-tied.

"There'll be other royals there. And ambassadors and delegates, all of whom you're used to, I'm sure, but our house isn't a castle. It's fine, but it's probably nothing compared to yours. I mean, you might not want to come. I totally understand," she said.

"What? No, of course not. I'd love to come," said Bozo, who figured it was good manners to jump down and speak to her right side up.

"What about me and Oscar?" said Andre. Oscar, too, piped up with a tweet.

Aoife looked at him from head to toe. Her cold, frosty gaze said it all. "Of course you can come," she said. Her words were polite, but her tone suggested she didn't mean them. "We already have servants, Andre, but if you want to come along and help, that's fine with me."

Now Andre was the one who felt like a shy toddler. He looked at his friend to clarify the misunderstanding, but Bozo didn't mention that Andre was his friend, not his servant.

"Aoife!" Frederick called again from the car.

"I better go now," she said as she turned to leave.

"Wait ... where do you live?" asked Bozo.

Not wanting to shout it out in front of the

whole street, she called back, “Frederick will collect you from here, tomorrow at seven.”

She ran past Elvis, who shouted at her, “I haven’t given up on us, darling.”

She frowned and got into the car.

“Who was that?” asked her father.

“Oh, see that guy over there? That’s my boyfriend,” she replied proudly.

“What, the one being taken away by the gardaí?” he asked, confused

They both looked over at Bozo, Andre and Oscar, who were, in fact, being led away by the gardaí.

“Daddy, he’s a prince. They’re his bodyguards,” she reasoned. “He probably has some very urgent diplomatic matter to attend to, and the gardaí need to get him there straight away,” she explained. "It must be extremely important. I know everyone thinks it's easy being a royal, but they don't understand the responsibility." She fixed her hair as though preparing herself for her royal duties as girlfriend of Prince Bozo.

Dressed for Success

Andre and Oscar spent the remainder of the day at the garda station, where the two boys were warned to stay out of trouble and to stop doing such dangerous tricks on Grafton Street.

The boys walked home in the wind and rain. They were tired after such an eventful day.

“Can we get some shoes tomorrow, Bozo? I’m cold and my feet are soaking wet,” Andre said as they trudged along.

“No,” said Bozo, entranced by his thoughts of the following night. “I have to get a new suit. You heard Aoife: this party is going to be full of kings and queens and diplomats and delegates.

I'm going to have to dress like a prince."

Andre was very disappointed, not to mention cold.

"Besides, Andre, I'm doing this so that we can get home and find our families. That's what you want, isn't it?"

Andre nodded. Of course, that was what they both wanted.

"What's a delegate?" Andre had never heard the word before.

"Delegates are things that are so fragile, you have to be careful not to break them," Bozo replied.

Andre was quite for a moment.

"Isn't that *delicate*?"

"No, Andre," Bozo said with a sigh, "it's delegates."

Andre was a little hurt, as he had been by Aoife's comment about him being a servant. But he didn't feel like arguing, as he was beginning to shiver and sneeze and his head was pounding.

That night, neither of the boys got much sleep, Bozo because of the party, and Andre because of his headache, which grew sorer, while his cough grew louder.

The next morning, Bozo was the only one who got out of bed.

"Bozo, I'm really sick. I can't get up," Andre moaned.

Bozo rolled his eyes up to heaven. "Andre, you're such a wimp sometimes."

Andre definitely didn't like the changes in his friend, even if it was all to get them home.

They were friends, and they had made a deal to look out for each other.

The following morning Bozo did his morning exercises, full of the joys of life. He put his hand into their tin box of money, although he knew he wasn't leaving much for the rest of the week.

"Where are you going?" asked Andre

"Well I can't wear these clothes tonight, can I? I'm going down to buy myself a suit," Bozo replied.

"A suit?" said Andre, lifting his sore head off the pillow. "But we don't have enough money, Bozo. And I think we're going to have to buy medicine for my sick."

"Andre, the word is *illness*," Bozo said condescendingly. "You'll be fine - it's just a cold."

Andre was really hurt that Bozo was being so mean.

"I'm not a wimp, Bozo. And I'm not stupid."

"Oh, grow up, Andre," said Bozo as he slammed the door behind him.

A few hours later, Bozo arrived home holding the top of a zippered hanging case.

"Hi, Andre! Wait until you see what I got. Aoife is going to love me in this," he said as he started to put it on.

Andre didn't lift his head off the pillow. "Bozo, I feel worse than I did this morning. I'm going to have to go to the doctor."

"Come on, you'll be fine. Think of all the lovely food we'll get to eat at this dinner."

"But Bozo, I ca -" Andre was cut off.

"One, two, three!" Bozo interrupted as he pulled the blankets off his bed.

Slowly, Andre got to his feet.

Bozo got dressed. He looked very smart in the black suit, white shirt, black dicky bow and shiny black shoes that he had bought in a second-hand shop but which looked like new. He made sure to pack his video recorder and batteries. This was his one opportunity to confront Sandy and go home and he wasn't about to mess it up.

"Don't I look like a prince?" asked Bozo, looking in the mirror, delighted with himself.

"No. You look like a penguin," Andre replied to his traitor of a friend.

Bozo was too busy admiring himself to notice, or even care, that Andre was annoyed.

"What am I going to wear?" asked Andre, looking at his dirty clothes and hole-ridden shoes. He thought he looked poor standing beside Bozo.

"The same thing you always wear, Andre. Don't worry, all the servants wear the same thing."

They looked at each other. Andre was disgusted. Even Bozo was disgusted with himself, but he didn't apologise.

"The word *servant* means *assistant* in Ireland," Bozo said, trying to cover his tracks. "And we had always agreed that you were my assistant. Besides, we're just doing this so that we can get home. This is important to both of us, Andre. We have to get home and find our parents. Stick with me on this. We're a team, okay?"

"I'm not your servant, Bozo," said Andre as they shut the door behind them.

Oh Me Oh My

The two boys and Oscar didn't speak as they walked to the bottom of Grafton Street to wait for their lift.

A long shiny black Mercedes Benz with dark windows and a cream leather interior awaited them. A man in a black suit with a black cap and white gloves held the door open as they approached.

Bozo walked past the driver with his nose pointed to the sky, without acknowledging him. He was more like his grandmother than he thought.

"Thank you," said Andre, accompanied by a

tweet from Oscar, neither of whom had forgotten their manners.

The fifteen-minute drive to Aoife's house was like a journey into another world. Looking left and right, the boys were in awe of the huge mansions and massive cars they saw. This was certainly a side to Dublin they never knew existed. The car turned towards the biggest house of them all, surrounded by an enormous wall protected by cameras and a security team. The gates opened and they drove along a gravelled driveway that was dotted with lights and security men. There were four enormous pillars outside the front door. Andre counted twenty-eight windows in the front of the house. Stepping out of the car and climbing the steps, the two boys looked up at the enormous black wooden door. This place was nicer than any hotel or yacht either of them had seen. Bozo quickly shook off his awe and wonderment. He tried to conceal the fact that he was impressed in case Aoife was watching him from the house and realised that this was not something he was used to. And this was something all princes ought to be used to.

I've been to things like this before, thought Bozo. It was true. He had attended similar events back home, only he was the one holding the door or handing out the drinks or polishing the cutlery.

The music of a string quartet near the doorway gently set the atmosphere for the party.

If Bozo's grandmother prepared him for high society, then Aoife defined everything she had imagined it to be.

Walking into the house, they were greeted by Mr. Jim Stephenson, a tall, larger-than-life character with lots of charisma, no hair and a massive belly.

"Good evening, gentlemen. You must be Prince Bozo, and you're ... you're ..." He didn't know how to address Andre.

"That's his servant, Father," said Aoife sharply as she walked up him. "Run along over there with the others. People will need their drinks,"

Andre looked at Bozo, waiting for him to correct the misunderstanding.

"Yes, Andre, pull your weight. You know how this is done."

Andre stared at Bozo. Before he could shout, "I am not a servant! That woman is a liar! Where are our families? Get us home *now*!" Brains grabbed him by the arm.

"Come on, sunshine," he said, as he escorted him to the kitchen, "you're with us."

"Care for a drink, sir?" asked a familiar voice. Bozo turned and saw Elvis dressed in a waiter's uniform. "A Prince not defending his staff is poor form. Bad quality in someone if you ask me," he whispered in Bozo's ear, while Aoife and her father chatted.

"What are you doing here?" asked Bozo.

"You don't think I'd give up a fight for Aoife that easily to you? Aoife and I go back a long way," Elvis answered.

"Bozo," said Aoife, grabbing him by the arm. "It's very nice of you to talk to the staff," she murmured as she walked him over to her father.

“This is my beautiful fiancée, Lady Sandy, Aoife’s new mother,” said Mr. Stephenson proudly.

“She is not my mother; she will never be my mother,” said Aoife very firmly.

Mr. Stephenson and Lady Sandy laughed off the awkwardness of what Aoife had said.

“Lady Sandy is a royal also, an English royal,” Jim continued.

At last, Bozo came face to face with Sandy. There she was, the woman who had taken Mr. Edwards’ money and left him with only heartache. She had also taken Bozo’s dream. If it wasn’t for her, his family would be in America now, living like superstars.

On seeing Bozo, the blood drained from Sandy’s

face. Her crystal glass slipped momentarily but she caught it just in time to avoid a spectacle. She stood frozen, looking at him in disbelief. Thousands of miles away from Vladislav, she had met Bozo - the only person in this very important house, with all these very important people - who knew the truth about her.

“Pleased to meet you,” she said, beaming her hundred-watt smile. She composed herself very quickly and slipped back into character.

“Oh, what Royal line are you from?” asked Bozo. Everybody looked to Sandy for an answer, including Mr. Stephenson, who had never thought to ask this question before. Sandy shot daggers at Bozo with her eyes.

“You might be related,” said Mr. Stephenson trying to ease the awkward tension.

"Dad and Sandy are getting married next week. That makes me a royal, doesn't it?" Aoife asked, hoping beyond hope that the answer was still yes.

"Yes, darling Aoife. It's the same answer as yesterday and the day before and the day before that," said her dad wearily.

"Let me show you some of my paintings," said Mr. Stephenson to the guests who had gathered in the entrance hall. As they walked towards the grand marble staircase, Bozo felt himself being pulled away and suddenly he was in a dark closet with the door closed behind him. There was only a faint light, which shone clearly into Sandy's face.

"What the hell are you doing here? Did the police send you? Are you a spy?" she asked, holding him tightly by the neck of his shirt.

"What the hell are *you* doing here, *Lady* Sandy?" he said back, not afraid of her.

"You'd better stay out of my way," she said. "I never, ever want to see you again. Is that clear?

"Not so easy, Lady Sandy," said Bozo. "You see, you didn't cover your tracks enough. I have evidence of what you did to Mr. Edwards and how you used his money for guns for the war."

"What did I do to Mr. Edwards?" she asked with a worried look on her face.

"It's all here," he said as he lifted up his video camera to show her the clip where she was speaking to her husband in the circus tent and outside the truck the night he escaped.

Her face froze again and she took her hand off Bozo's shirt.

"How much do you want?" she said as though money would get rid of them.

"I don't want money. I want you to find my family in Vladislav and get us home safely," he replied.

"But Vladislav is at war. How do you expect me to do that?" she asked.

"A war that you and your people have caused. You started the war. You will know where my family is," Bozo responded.

"This is ridiculous. I can't believe I'm being blackmailed by a child," she said.

"The quicker you get us home, the quicker we are out of your hair and you can go on living your pretend life," said Bozo.

"I'm won't be threatened by you," said Sandy.

"Then I will tell everyone tonight; your

reputation will be in ruins. Oh, and by the way, Andre has a copy too, ready to be played to the entire room. So you have two choices: work with us or against us." Bozo called her bluff. Andre didn't have a copy, but he only had one chance at this and he needed to frighten Sandy enough to get her to help them.

Bozo played the video to her.

"Okay, okay, I will get my people working on it." she said. "But leave when I tell you to ... or else."

"Sandy, honey, where are you," called Mr. Stephenson. Sandy soon joined him.

Bozo felt quite important that the best seat in the house was reserved for him, and as he sat he noticed a lot of attention from the other guests.

"Would you take my grave as quickly?" asked Aoife's dad, laughing. Elvis had swapped Bozo's place card and put him at the top table, in the biggest chair saved for Mr. Stephenson. Table plan or no table plan, this was something that anyone used to this type of company would have been familiar with.

"First, he's taking my daughter, now he's taking my job," he said in front of all the guests, who found it quite entertaining that this boy was committing the cardinal sin of sitting at the head of the table at someone else's party. However, Mr. Stephenson smoothed over the mistake like a true gentleman.

"It's because he's a prince and normally princes sit at the head of the table. He's just not used to being down here," said Aoife, proud as a peacock as she explained the perfectly valid reason for the mix up. It seemed that everything Bozo did impressed her more.

Bozo was relieved to finally make it to the correct seat. But Elvis had mixed up the order of Bozo's table setting, so Bozo didn't know which of the three forks and three knives and three spoons to use.

"Oh, in our country we work from the outside in," Aoife said to him quietly, realising that customs where he came from might be different.

Relieved, and just delighted to have a hot dinner, Bozo started to eat his soup with his fork.

The End of the Evening

"Pleasure to meet you, what a very pleasant evening," said Bozo, who was learning the lingo of high society so quickly that even his accent was beginning to change.

Aoife rang a bell, which called all the waiting staff to collect their wages for the evening.

Andre walked past them without uttering a word.

"Won't you join me tomorrow for some polo in the park?" Aoife asked Bozo

Polo? thought Bozo.

"There are lots of riding boots and hats there and you can borrow one of my horses, Camelot.

We can collect you at your ... palace? Where are you staying, by the way?"

"In a fridge!" shouted Andre.

"Oh, he's so funny. Andre can't get used to the Irish weather, so he thinks everywhere is cold," Bozo explained.

Aoife looked at Andre again and he was indeed shivering in the car. "Yes, look, he's even cold now."

But Andre was becoming sicker and sicker and, for the first time in a while, Bozo was beginning to feel bad. "Take my jacket to warm yourself up," said Bozo as he took off his jacket and handed it to Andre. But Andre was so angry with Bozo that he wouldn't accept it.

"I can organise for my driver to collect you in the morning. You can bring your parents," said

Aoife.

"Oh no, they won't be there tomorrow," replied Bozo.

"Okay," said Aoife, looking a little disappointed.

"But I can be there if you like," said Bozo.

"Great, I'll get my driver to collect you at the same spot," she offered.

Bozo agreed. Besides, he needed to stay close to Aoife so that Sandy would tell him when they could get home.

He was beginning to feel a twinge of guilt that he knew all of this about Sandy, yet he couldn't tell Aoife. That night, Bozo and Andre went to bed. The only noise in the room all night was Andre's coughing.

The next morning, Bozo took the last money

they had out of the savings tin to pay for his daytime clothes. He left while Andre was still sleeping.

Life Is a Game

Bozo pulled up to the polo grounds at the Phoenix Park in the chauffeur-driven black Mercedes.

Luckily, he was used to grooming horses in his village at home, so he was a dab hand at putting on their bridles and saddles and measuring their stirrups. He just wasn't that used to riding them with a saddle. He was more used to riding bareback, just jumping on and holding on to the mane for dear life.

One, two, three, he hopped up. Terrified, he swayed forwards and back as he crouched forward, holding on to the horse's mane.

Fearless and afraid of nobody, he thought as he sat upright and hoped to make it through the day without Aoife suspecting anything.

“You’re a very private prince, Bozo. Is it okay if I call you Bozo?” asked Aoife.

“Sure, I’d prefer that. It makes me feel more at home,” replied Bozo.

“What are your parents like?” she asked

Aoife had hit a sore point. Bozo had thought he would be able to talk about them, but when it came to it, he couldn’t say much.

“My father is a real free spirit. He has very unique way of looking at things. He loves nature and the circus and people. My mother ... my mother is very kind,” Bozo’s voice was beginning to break. He tried to hold it together, but reminiscing about home was something he hadn't done in a few days.

"Do you have any friends?" she asked Bozo.

Bozo thought about Andre. This should be an easy question to answer. "No, I don't have any friends." Bozo felt terrible as soon as the words were out. He felt a lump in his throat. He had gone too far.

"What about Andre? He seems a little ... I didn't think a prince would hang around with a boy like ... he's not exactly ..."

"He's not exactly what?" asked Prince Bozo.

"The best?" she said boldly.

"Tell me about your family," asked Bozo, wanting to change the subject.

"Well, my mother died two years ago and things just haven't been the same since," she said sadly. "My dad and I were really close after it happened and he really looked out for me. Anyway, a while ago, he met Sandy ... and, well, I don't like her and he has definitely changed. We never spend any time together and she is always demanding his full attention. Plus she's always really nice to me when he's there, but really not nice to me when he's not. Everyone thinks it's because she's not my mother and I'm jealous and I need to be happy for my father. And I am. I just ... I don't know. I just don't trust her, Bozo."

"Um," said Bozo. At this point he felt very bad about himself. He wanted to tell Aoife about Sandy, but then he would have to tell her how he knew and he just couldn't bring himself to do it.

"Plus, they're getting married in a few weeks.

And then that'll be that. They'll probably have more kids and I'll be forgotten about." And I don't have any friends anymore.'

"Why not?"

"Well, I'm not from here. I used to live in another part of Dublin; you wouldn't know it. I used to be friends with Elvis and Sniffer and Brains. I used to be in their gang but that all changed when I moved house and, well, I don't have any friends from school. I'm starting at a boarding school in Switzerland in a few weeks, so what's the point in making new friends when I won't be here? You're my only friend, Bozo; I really trust you."

This made Bozo feel even worse. He knew so much about Sandy and knew she was going take Mr. Stephenson's money and break his heart, yet he could do nothing to stop it. Well, he could, but it would mean not getting home to see his family.

"They're going on a pre-honeymoon in a few days," continued Aoife.

"A what?" asked Bozo. He had never heard of that before. It must be a high-society thing.

"A honeymoon before they get married, because they're so in love. And clearly I wasn't invited."

"Come on, Bozo, let's get moving." Aoife whipped Camelot on his hindquarters and they both galloped through the woods. Bozo held on to the reins for dear life.

Cometh the Hour, Cometh the Man

Bozo returned home from his lovely day at the polo grounds. He had been treated to the finest food and he had even managed to sneak some tasty biscuits and sandwiches into his bag for Andre.

Opening the door, he called out to Andre.

"Andre, look what I brought you back. You have to taste these cookies; they're delicious."

Andre was still in the bed. Bozo looked up and saw Oscar by his side, still as statue, resting on the windowsill above Andre's bed. Bozo had always known Oscar to be full of life, but not only was he not moving, the colour of his body was a very dark grey, almost black.

“Andre! Wake up, Andre,” Bozo shouted in a panic, but there was no movement. Bozo ran to his bed and shook his body.

“Andre, please wake up! Andre, please!” But Andre’s didn’t move.

“AAAAAAANNNNNNDREEEEE!” screamed Bozo.

“AAAAAAANNNNNNDREEEEE!” he screamed over and over again.

“Somebody help,” he yelled.

Bozo looked up at Oscar, who remained still.

“Oscar, don’t just sit there. Do something.” But Oscar didn’t move.

“Oscar, please. Please, Oscar, do something!” He screamed into Oscar’s face, but Oscar remained still.

Bozo needed help but he couldn’t call the

gardaí.

He needed to tell someone, and fast.

He ran out the door and onto the street, where he met Elvis and his gang.

“Well, look what we have here,” said Elvis, ready for the next chapter in his battle.

Breathless and terrified, Bozo said, “Guys, you have to help me. Andre, he’s sick. He’s so sick he might die.”

“Is there nobody in the palace to help you?” asked Elvis sarcastically.

“Seriously, he is going to die and you have to help me. We can’t bring him to hospital or to the police because we’ll be sent home to fight in the war,” he pleaded.

“No way. You’re the enemy,” said Elvis.

“But he might die” said Brains, who realised

how serious this was. “We need to bring him to Aoife’s,” he said quickly thinking of a solution.

“We don’t owe this guy anything,” said Elvis coldly.

“This is serious. If you help me bring him to Aoife’s, I will admit that I am not a royal and that I am poor and you should be Aoife’s boyfriend and not me. At least you have been true to yourself, Elvis. You’re not pretending to be somebody else and at least you know who your friends are. Not like me, I had the best friend anyone could wish for and I betrayed him. The only reason Aoife wanted me to be her boyfriend was that she thought I was something I’m not”.

“We can get a taxi to Aoife’s house. She’ll have a doctor there and he will look after Andre,” said Brains who had come to like Andre the night they were all working at Aoife's house.

"I have some money. I can hail a big taxi that can bring us all to Aoife's house," said Sniffer.

"Okay, let's do it," said Elvis.

"I owe you for this," said Bozo, relieved.

Never a Truer Word Spoken

They carried Andre out and put him in the back of the taxi. Bozo felt awful about himself. How could he have been so stupid? Why was everyone else sorting this out and not him?

"Is Aoife here?" they asked the security man who was sitting in his cabin at the front gate of her house.

He pressed a button, as though ringing her phone. The boys could see her up in her room answering the phone.

"Miss Aoife, there's some ..." he looked them up and down, "people here to see you."

She looked out the window. Bozo was standing

outside the car, looking up at her hopefully.

“What’s your name?” asked the security man.

“Bozo,” he replied.

“Ok, go on in,” said the security man. He opened the black steel gates and the taxi drove the boys up to the front door of the house.

Aoife opened the large wooden front door.

“Hi Prince Bozo,” Aoife said cheerfully to Bozo when she opened the door. Her face suddenly became very serious as she watched Bozo carry Andre out of the taxi with Elvis, Sniffer and Brains following behind.

“What’s going on?” asked Aoife looking very concerned.

“Aoife, Andre is very sick and he needs to see a doctor straight away.”

“What? I don’t understand. And what are *they*

doing here?" said Aoife pointing at Elvis, Sniffer and Brains.

The boys had all gathered inside the front door of Aoife's house. "Aoife, I haven't been honest with you. I am not royalty, well not in the way you think that we are. We have escaped the war in Vladislav and we are very poor. We need your help. Andre needs to see a doctor very soon or he will die."

"You lied to me?" asked Aoife, stunned.

"Yes Aoife I lied to you, because I knew that if you thought I was poor you wouldn't want to know me," replied Bozo.

"That's not true," said Aoife.

"Isn't that the reason you don't want to be friends with us anymore?" asked Elvis.

Aoife said nothing, she just lowered her head.

“Aoife, I have nothing. I have no family, no money and now I am losing my best friend. None of this rich/poor stuff matters. None of it. Elvis, Sniffer, Brains they’re your friends. Even I’m your friend. Cherish what you have, Aoife, because tomorrow morning you may have nothing. Now please can we get a doctor to see Andre,” begged Bozo raising his voice.

Aoife looked at each of the boys and then looked at Andre and said, “Okay put him in the front room. I’ll get my father.”

“What’s all this about?” bellowed Mr. Stephenson’s as he marched into the room a few moments later.

“Sir, I am very sorry sir. I need you to help my friend Andre. He is dying,” pleaded Bozo.

Jim placed his hand on Andre’s forehead and

checked his pulse before shouting to the house staff that had followed him into the room. “Call a doctor this minute!”

“Thank you, sir,” said Bozo his eyes filling up with tears.

“Okay, son. Aoife has told me your story. You are a brave boy. Fearless I would say. Fearless and afraid of nobody,” said Aoife’s father.

“Thank you, sir,” replied Bozo, his voice breaking with emotion. “That’s what my father used to say”.

“You’re in safe hands now, my boy. We’ll take it from here. Now you boys go to the kitchen and chef will fix you some food,” said Mr. Stephenson.

Bozo was the last of the boys to walk out of the room. He paused, took his video recorder out of his top pocket and walked back to Mr. Stephenson.

“Sir, you need to see this,” said Bozo leaving the video recorder on the table beside the door.

Hope

Bozo had finished eating his food and Elvis, Sniffer and Brains were sent home.

The doctor had arrived and was taking care of Andre. Bozo and Aoife were allowed into the room after a few hours to see how he was doing.

“He’s not going to die, is he?” asked Aoife.

Bozo’s mother had always told Bozo that when someone is dying, they could still hear every word that was spoken and he didn’t want to worry Andre.

Bozo responded quickly, “Of course he’s not going to die. He’s just a little sick. We all get sick."

Oscar was standing on the top of the headboard behind Andre, still motionless and still dark in colour.

The doctor looked at them both and signaled to get them to go outside. They followed the doctor to the other room.

"Well?" they asked.

"I'm afraid the news isn't good."

"How bad?" asked Bozo.

"Bozo, I'm afraid your friend may not make it," replied the doctor.

"He *will* make it. He has made it this far. He is a lot stronger and a lot better than anyone knows. Besides, he's my friend. He's my only family now. I have lost everyone else and I am not losing him," said Bozo.

Bozo charged back into the room. Maybe it was anger; maybe it was a last ditch attempt to hold on to the one thing he had left in his life; Maybe it was a mixture of everything, but Bozo wasn't going to leave Andre's side until he got better. "Hey, Andre. How are you doing? I just wanted to let you know that the rain has stopped, and guess what? It's snowing outside." Bozo took his friend's cool hand.

"I've asked God to make it snow again when you're better so that we can make snowmen like you always wanted." Wiping a tear from his eye, Bozo forced his voice to remain steady. "I'll practice with Aoife until you get better. Wait until you see her whole house, Andre. It's like a palace. They've got servants and maids and a tennis court and a swimming pool."

None of the wealth around him made any impact anymore. The only thing that Bozo wished was for his friend to live.

“Keep going, Andre. You’re the strongest fighter and the best friend I know. Besides, Oscar couldn’t live without you. You need to fight for our sakes. You have to.”

Over the next few days Bozo continued to talk to Andre like normal. Aoife and Bozo played cards. They each took turns laying the cards on the bed, dealing Andre’s hand as though he was playing.

Bozo and Aoife refused to leave the room. They slept with their heads on Andre’s bed. Bozo knew that Andre could hear every word and every so often he would break into a pantomime that had always made Andre laugh, but Andre remained asleep.

“Bozo,” said Mr. Stephenson as he walked into the room, waking Bozo and Aoife from their sleep early in the morning.

“I have some good news, son. The war is over and we have located your family. Andre’s mother and your parents and grandmother are alive.”

“Bozo, I’m hungry,” said Andre weakly as he opened his eyes.

“Of course you’re hungry. You’ve been asleep for days, you lazy sod,” replied Bozo, wiping the tears from his eyes.

“Look, Bozo, we can make snowman now,” said Andre looking out the window to the snow outside.

Happiness

Mr. Stephenson organised for a special private jet to bring the boys and Oscar home. Aoife, Elvis, Sniffer and Brains came with them on a minibus to say goodbye.

"We'll write to you when we get back to Vladislav," said Bozo to his new friends, ready to board the plane. "Yeah, maybe we'll meet again someday," said Elvis.

"I haven't given up on being a circus superstar," said Bozo. "Maybe you could join us on our world tour," he said with a laugh, but with a hint of seriousness, too.

"You bet," said Elvis.

"Thanks for saving my life," said Andre, and Oscar tweeted in agreement.

Bozo Andre and Oscar ran onto the plane so eager were they to get home.

Once they arrived in Vladislav there was a driver to meet them to bring them to their families.

Andre, Bozo and Oscar's hearts pounded with excitement once they spotted the familiar scenery of Port Alexandrov. "We're home, Andre. We're home! Can you believe it?"

"We said we'd beat the war, Andre, and we did. We're heroes," said Bozo, unable to contain his excitement as he started jumping up and down.

They drove to the old town and the boys opened the car door where they felt the heat of the sun as though it was giving them a hug.

"We're home! We're home! We're home! We're home!" the boys jumped around with joy.

"Come with me," said the driver as the boys and Oscar followed him up the steps of a narrow street and into a house at the top of a windy set of stone steps. Oscar's wings couldn't have shone more brightly.

They all piled into the small dark kitchen that had one small window, an oven and lots of chairs. It was very humble in comparison to Aoife's home, but there was no other house in the world that Bozo, Andre and Oscar would rather be in.

"Mama, Mama," cried Bozo and Andre as they both embraced their mothers, Franjo,

Grandmother and Mr. Edwards. This moment was too extraordinary for words. It was as though heaven itself had wrapped its arms around them.

The evening was spent laughing and singing and each person recounted stories of what had happened to them since they had been separated. Bozo and Andre recounted the months of survival in Dublin and everyone was in awe at how they managed to stay alive and come back home to their families.

That night, Bozo climbed into his own bed in a house filled with his own family, in his own country. And he had the best friend he could ever wish for.

I have everything I could ever want, thought Bozo. *I really am a prince.*

Made in the USA
Charleston, SC
12 February 2014